THE GUNSMITH

#56

WALKING DEAD MAN

The Gunsmith by J.R. Roberts

Macklin's Women
The Chinese Gunmen
The Woman Hunt
The Guns of Abilene
Three Guns for Glory
Leadtown
The Longhorn War
Quanah's Revenge
Heavyweight Gun
New Orleans Fire
One-Handed Gun
The Canadian Payroll
Draw to an Inside Death
Dead Man's Hand
Bandit Gold
Buckskins and Six-Guns
Silver War
High Noon at Lancaster
Bandido Blood
The Dodge City Gang
Sasquatch Hunt
Bullets and Ballots
The Riverboat Gang
Killer Grizzly
North of the Border
Eagle's Gap
Chinatown Hell
The Panhandle Search
Wildcat Roundup
The Ponderosa War
Trouble Rides a Fast Horse
Dynamite Justice
The Posse
Night of the Gila
The Bounty Women
Black Pearl Saloon
Gundown in Paradise
King of the Border
The El Paso Salt War
The Ten Pines Killer
Hell with a Pistol
Wyoming Cattle Kill
The Golden Horseman
The Scarlet Gun
Navaho Devil

Wild Bill's Ghost
The Miner's Showdown
Archer's Revenge
Showdown in Raton
When Legends Meet
Desert Hell
The Diamond Gun
Denver Duo
Hell on Wheels
The Legend Maker
Walking Dead Man
Crossfire Mountain
The Deadly Healer
The Trail Drive War
Geronimo's Trail
The Comstock Gold Fraud
Boom Town Killer
Texas Trackdown
The Fast Draw League
Showdown in Rio Malo
Outlaw Trail
Homesteader Guns
Five Card Death
Trail Drive to Montana
Trial by Fire
The Old Whistler Gang
Daughter of Gold
Apache Gold
Plains Murder
Deadly Memories
The Nevada Timber War
New Mexico Showdown
Barbed Wire and Bullets
Death Express
When Legends Die
Six Gun Justice
The Mustang Hunters
Texas Ransom
Vengeance Town
Winner Take All
Message from a Dead Man
Ride for Vengeance
The Takersville Shoot
Blood On the Land
Six-Gun Sideshow

THE GUNSMITH

#56

WALKING DEAD MAN

J.R. ROBERTS

SPEAKING VOLUMES, LLC
NAPLES, FLORIDA
2014

THE GUNSMITH
#56 WALKING DEAD MAN

ISBN 978-1-61232-659-7

Chapter One

Clint Adams had just spent a very profitable month in Indian Territory. His ability to fix almost any gun, no matter what was wrong with it—and Indian Territory was the place to find guns, all shapes and sizes, suffering from all kinds of disorders —guaranteed a good income.

He was in Texas now, trying to make up his mind just which direction to take. Should he head south, back to Labyrinth for some rest and relaxation, or should he head east or west, looking for more business? Suddenly, in the town of Northfield, over breakfast, the question resolved itself.

The man who entered the dining room was tall, light-haired, slender. He was blinking his eyes rapidly, as if the light hurt them. Clint guessed he'd hit town late last night and had only just gotten up. He waited patiently to see how alert the man would be, and whether or not he would spot Clint.

The man started in his direction without any indication of having seen him. He seemed about to walk *past* him to an unoccupied table when suddenly he stopped and put his hand on Clint's shoulder, squeezing hard.

1

"I'll bet you thought I was too tired to see you," the man said with a smile.

Clint smiled back and said, "Hello, Wyatt."

"How the hell are you, Clint?" Wyatt Earp said, sitting down opposite the Gunsmith. "Still putting away big breakfasts, I see—with two pots of coffee?"

"This is my first. Help yourself."

Invariably when Clint told a waiter that he was going to want two pots of coffee, one after the other, a second cup materialized on the table. It was as if they figured that a man ordering two pots of coffee must be expecting company.

Wyatt picked up the second cup and poured himself a full ration of coffee. He had added a leonine mustache, a great, sweeping thing, since they'd last seen each other. Clint guessed that Wyatt must have been twenty-nine by now, but except for the mustache he looked much the same as ever.

"I need this."

"Late night?"

"The latest. I could have stopped and camped but I wanted to make Northfield so I'd be here this morning."

A Mexican waiter came over and Wyatt ordered a duplicate of Clint's breakfast, eggs, spuds, bacon and biscuits.

"Two pots of coffee, Señor?" the man asked.

"We'll work on mine and, if need be, go to a third," Clint said.

"As you say, Señor."

Wyatt took a healthy, grateful gulp of the steaming hot black coffee and then asked, "Are you coming or going?"

"Passing through. Just got out of Indian Territory and I'm picking a direction."

"Maybe I can interest you in mine."

"What are you up to, these days?"

"Railroad detective."

"Hunting?"

Wyatt nodded.

"Man named Rudabaugh held up a Sante Fe train in Kansas. They hired me to find him and bring him back, along with the money he stole."

"Is he alone?"

"No way of telling."

"But you are."

Wyatt nodded.

"Can't get anyone but you or Bat to ride with me. Can't stand anyone else."

"Nobody else can stand you, you mean."

"That's what I mean."

Bat was their mutual friend, Bat Masterson and, although both he and Wyatt were younger than Clint, their reputations had grown to almost rival his own. He'd watched their fame grow since he'd first met them, with a mixture of fear and pride. Now they'd have to start looking over their shoulders and sitting with their backs against the wall to guard against backshooters. He had caught them when he wished someone had caught him, but it hadn't done any good. They had both gone ahead and followed the same general path that he had, and maybe theirs —and his—had been unavoidable. Maybe it had all been mapped out way in advance, with nothing any-one could do to stop it . . . .

"I've been following your progress, you know. You and Bat, both."

"Long way from buffalo hunting, huh?" Wyatt asked, referring to what he and Bat had been doing when they first met Clint Adams.[1]

"You fellas seem to be doing it right."

"You mean we've kept our reps on the side of the law, so far. We learned that from you."

"You didn't need me to teach you that."

"It didn't hurt, meeting you that early on."

"What's Bat up to?"

Wyatt shrugged.

"Last I heard he was a Sheriff in Ford County while his brother Ed was Marshal of Dodge City. Could still be that way, for all I know. I'll be heading back to Dodge after I've taken care of Rudabaugh."

"Never heard of this fella before," Clint said.

"Dave Rudabaugh. A bad one, Clint. Fast with a gun I hear tell."

"They're all fast with a gun."

"Ain't that the truth."

Wyatt's breakfast came and both men set about devouring their food. Clint, having started first, finished first and began the second pot of coffee.

"So?" Wyatt said after he was finished.

"So what?"

"Want to come along?"

"Where you headed?"

"South, to Fort Griffin, in Shackelford County."

"You figure he headed there?"

"That's where most of them head, ain't it? I heard it's a bad place."

"Ask John Selman."

John Selman had been a Deputy Sheriff of

[1]THE GUNSMITH #5: THREE GUNS FOR GLORY

Shackelford County until he had been exposed as one of the area's biggest stock thieves.

"I heard. If they could run a man like Selman out I guess they must be pretty tough there, huh?"

"Too tough for one man, I guess," Clint said. "Even you."

"Or you?"

"Maybe."

"Only one way to find out."

Since Labyrinth was on the way to Fort Griffin, Clint decided to go ahead and ride along with his friend. They could make a short stop to drop off his rig and then ride on to Fort Griffin.

"I guess I'd better tag along with you and keep you out of trouble."

"The way I remember it, trouble sort of follows you around, don't it?"

"Only when I'm with you or Masterson."

"Wouldn't life be dull without friends?" Wyatt asked.

Clint nodded. He knew that Wyatt didn't count many men as his friend, and he appreciated being one of them, even if it did usually mean trouble.

Ah well, it *had* been a peaceful month . . .

They finished out their day separately, Clint getting what relaxation he could while he could, and Wyatt checking up on Rudabaugh's progress by telegraph message. They met for dinner. Wyatt told Clint that his hunch seemed to have been right, that the word was that Dave Rudabaugh was indeed headed for Fort Griffin.

"Well, we'd better have a few drinks, play a little cards and get to bed, then," Clint said. "We'll have to start out early in the morning."

"I'm for cards and bed," Wyatt said, "as long as there's a young lady in this town to share the bed with."

"You need rest, Wyatt."

"I need a little company, Clint, and no offense meant, but yours isn't exactly what I had in mind."

"Well, you young fellas, that's all you think about," Clint said. "Me, I'm hitting my hotel room early. I need all the rest I can get if I'm going to be able to keep up with you."

"You still riding Duke?"

"Of course."

"Hell, that beast of yours could keep up with the Devil even if you was asleep in the saddle."

Clint grinned and said, "And many's the time that *he* has—and I was!"

Chapter Two

They got an early start in the morning and, from the smug, self-satisfied look on the younger man's face, Clint assumed that Wyatt had been successful in his search for some company.

They reached Labyrinth at midday and decided to stay over and start out again in the morning. Clint introduced Wyatt to Rick Hartman, who was sufficiently impressed to offer the services of his saloon on the house—including the women. Wyatt took full advantage of the situation. Clint took one of the women back to his hotel with him as well.

Once they left Labyrinth and headed for Fort Griffin in search of Dave Rudabaugh, there was no telling what would happen. Clint felt—and he knew that Wyatt felt the same way—there was always a chance that they wouldn't reach Fort Griffin alive, or that they wouldn't leave it, which would make this night the last such night they'd spend on this earth.

A sobering thought, but one that men like Clint Adams, Wyatt Earp, and Bat Masterson had lived with and—as in the case of Wild Bill Hickok—would probably eventually die with.

•   •   •

Dave Rudabaugh, saddlebags bulging with the money he had stolen from the Sante Fe train, sat atop his roan and stared down at Fort Griffin and the town surrounding it, which was generally known as the "Flat."

He was tired and he was irritable. He hadn't had a chance to stop and spend any of the money he'd stolen. Friends had tipped him off that the railroad had put Wyatt Earp on his trail. Rudabaugh knew Earp's reputation and the news alarmed him. Himself a fast man with a gun, he knew Earp's rep as a gunman and as a lawman. As soon as he'd heard he'd set off for Fort Griffin. He knew some people there—some friends, some not. If he was going to make a stand against Wyatt Earp, that was the place to do it.

And he would make a stand, because he had no intention of spending the rest of his life on the run. He would kill Earp. Then, by the time the railroads got anyone else to try and pick up his trail, it would be stone cold.

Rudabaugh didn't know where he would end up —Mexico, South America, even Europe—but wherever it was he was going to have all that money, and all the time in the world to spend it.

All he had to do was stop Wyatt Earp.

There was a man in Fort Griffin who was not known to Wyatt Earp, Clint Adams or Dave Rudabaugh. Oh, they would know his reputation upon hearing his name, but none of them had ever met him. Ostensibly a dentist, the man was better known as a gambler, and even better known as a killer. Once the personalities of Wyatt Earp, Clint Adams and Dave Rudabaugh were put in contact with his own, there was no telling what the outcome might be.

The unsuspecting man's name was John Henry Holliday.

They called him "Doc".

Chapter Three

The Flat below Fort Griffin, which had been erected on the top of a low, flat hill, put even Dodge City and Deadwood to shame for pure meanness and wildness. The fort itself sat on Government Hill, while the town was simply the flat that surrounded it.

The Flat was the central trading point for cattlemen two hundred miles west. It was also the headquarters for a veritable army of buffalo hunters and a supply point on the overland cattle trail between southern Texas and Kansas.

Ramshackle houses had been erected to meet the needs of the Flat's growing populace. Ricks covered with buffalo hides, waiting to be shipped to Dallas or Fort Worth, 200 miles away, covered the spaces between the buildings.

Just outside the town was a camp for the army's Tonkawa Scouts, who were needed as the Comanches and Kiowas still made midnight raids. The scouts, cowhands, buffalo hunters and teamsters who visited the Flat were tough, all right, but so were the permanent residents of the settlement—the women as well as the men.

Wyatt Earp and Clint Adams rode through the

Flat on Griffin Street, which soon sloped up to take them to the Fort itself.

"I want to check in with the army first," Wyatt had said as they'd approached the town. "It always helps when trouble comes around if you've already told them of your presence."

"And we're expecting trouble to come around."

"It always does."

Clint shook his head and followed Wyatt into the piss-poor excuse for a town called by many Fort Griffin when it was actually known to all as the Flat.

Clint and Wyatt were shown in to the office of the fort commander, Colonel Charles L. Grant. Both men were surprised at the man's apparent youth. He looked to be in his mid-to-late thirties. A West Pointer, no doubt.

"Mr. Earp, Mr. Adams," Grant said, rising from behind his desk but declining to offer his hand.

"Colonel." Wyatt was the one who spoke and Clint remained silent, deferring to the fact that it was on Wyatt's business that they were in Fort Griffin. Wyatt removed his hat, but Clint kept his on.

"What can I do for you . . . gentlemen?"

"I'm in the employ of the railroad, Colonel, as this letter will attest." Wyatt produced a letter and handed it to the Colonel, who read it.

"I see. You're a railroad detective."

"That's right."

"And what brings you here?"

"I'm tracking a man who held up a Sante Fe train and made off with forty thousand dollars of payroll money."

"And you believe the man to be here in Fort Griffin?"

"More to the point, I believe he's down below, in the Flat somewhere."

"And his name?"

"Dave Rudabaugh."

"I'm afraid I never heard of him," Grant said, handing the letter back, as if the statement should terminate their meeting.

"I didn't expect you would, Colonel. I'm here simply on a courtesy call, to let you know that I might be around for a few days until I can determine whether or not Rudabaugh is here, or has been here."

"And this man?" Colonel Grant indicated Clint with a slight inclination of his head. "Is he a railroad detective, as well?"

"No, he's not. Mr. Adams is a friend of mine who has agreed to lend me a hand."

Grant frowned at them and clasped his hands behind his back, puffing his chest out. Clint would have made a bet that the man was about to make some sort of declaration.

"I should tell you men that I'm well aware of your considerable reputations."

"What reputations are those, Colonel?" Clint asked.

Grant's frown deepened and he said, "As gunmen, as purveyors of trouble—"

"How about as lawmen?" Wyatt asked.

"Yes, as lawmen as well, but purveyors of trouble, nevertheless."

Clint figured the Colonel must have liked that

phrase to have repeated it so soon.

"Are you trying to tell us something?" Wyatt asked.

"Just that I won't tolerate trouble here, not from anyone."

"From what I've heard about the Flat, Colonel," Wyatt said, "you tolerate a hell of a lot of trouble. Is it just our brand of trouble that you object to, or is it just us in particular?"

"I have nothing against you . . . men personally," Grant said. "My main concern is with the smooth operation of this fort, and I won't tolerate any disruption. Is that understood?"

"We have no intention of disrupting your fort, Colonel . . . that is, unless Dave Rudabaugh is hiding somewhere inside of it."

"No one is hiding here, Mr. Earp, I can assure you," Grant said stiffly.

"That's fine," Wyatt said, replacing his hat, "then you and I won't have reason to cross swords, Colonel."

Wyatt started for the door and Clint moved away from the wall to follow him. On the way he spotted a small framed picture of Ulysses S. Grant adorning the wall. No, he thought, it couldn't be . . .

He turned to Colonel Grant and said, "Are you by any chance related?"

Grant looked at the picture and said, "Unfortunately, no, but I have tremendous respect for the man."

"So have I," Clint said, with satisfaction, and followed Wyatt out.

Wyatt and Clint were accompanied outside by the

Colonel's aide, a major and a veteran who obviously had ten or more years in the service than Grant did.

"Jackass," Wyatt said, loud enough for the aide to hear.

Clint looked at the man who simply grinned, nodded, and went back inside.

"Looks like there's some around here who would agree with you."

"More than some, I'd wager," Wyatt said, stepping down off the boardwalk. "Well, hopefully we won't have to talk to him again."

"I suppose we'd better go on down into the Flat and find a hotel."

"I'm not looking forward to that," Wyatt said. He looked at Clint and added, "At least I won't have to strain my eyes watching my own back."

"Go ahead and watch it," Clint said, "that'll make two of us."

Chapter Four

Big Nose Kate Elder had certainly earned her nickname, but her nose did nothing to keep her from being attractive to the opposite sex. Her face was pleasant and would have been pretty but for the nose, and her body was full and firm. Kate was an oddity among whores, as she worked for no one but herself, and owed allegiance to no house and no master.

Of late, however, she had taken herself off the streets and had become the private stock of one John Henry "Doc" Holliday. She had no idea how Doc felt about her, but she was crazy about him and would be his until he said different.

"It's a shame," Mike O'Brien said.

O'Brien was the owner of the Griffin Saloon against whose bar Kate was now leaning, watching while Doc went about his business, dealing faro.

"What is?"

"For you to take yourself out of circulation, Katie girl," O'Brien said. "Come on, how's about you and me going to my room while Doc is working?"

"Careful, Mike, or I'll tell Doc you suggested it."

"Jeez, Katie," O'Brien said, "I was only kidding, you know?"

17

Kate chuckled and said, "I know."

It was a game she played, invoking Doc's name whenever a man tried to get her to go back to work. She enjoyed watching them sweat, it gave her a feeling of power.

As she watched Doc now, a tall, slender, fair-haired man with sure hands, he was suddenly gripped by a staggering coughing fit. He grabbed for a handkerchief and held it to his mouth and Kate knew there was a good chance that there would be blood on it. She wanted to go to him, to hold him, but she knew that he didn't like that. It would make him feel weak. She wondered how long the consumption would take before it finally killed him, and how much it would take out of him between now and then.

No matter. She'd accept however much of Doc the sickness left her, until either it or Doc himself took him away from her.

At the livery Clint made sure that the liveryman knew what was expected of him. Even in a town like the Flat, however, good horseflesh was appreciated and the man promised to take special care of Duke. When the man asked Wyatt if he wanted the same care taken with his animal Wyatt said, "Just make sure he's alive and ready to move when I want him."

From there they went to the Griffin Hotel and checked in after changing the clerk's mind about having rooms available.

"You scared the poor lad to death," Clint scolded Wyatt as they climbed the stairs to their rooms.

"Hell, he figured he was gonna save the rooms for some high rollers."

"We can be high rollers."

"I'll take him up to the goddamn roof and roll him right off."

Wyatt's room overlooked the street and Clint's was right next to it. They stowed their gear and decided against trying to find a bath.

"With this town the water would probably be three days old and growing things, anyway," Wyatt said. "I'd rather have a drink."

"I'm for that."

They left the hotel and crossed the street to the saloon, which Wyatt had been able to see from his room.

"Jesus, this town stinks of buffalo hides," Wyatt said.

Clint hadn't been able to place the peculiar smell, but then he had never hunted buffalo the way Wyatt had.

"I'm glad I got out of that game."

"Saved up some money doing it, though."

"Sure," Wyatt said, "but that's all gone."

Clint knew that a lot of Wyatt's money had been spent trying to prolong his wife's life, but she had gone and died young, anyway. Wyatt never discussed that, though, so Clint didn't broach the subject.

It was still early in the day when they entered the saloon and they found it doing a brisk business, though not overcrowded. They both saw the faro dealer at the same time and looked at each other.

"Faro's not my game," Clint said.

"It is mine. I'll see you at the bar. I just want to try a few hands and test their dealer."

"Fine."

Clint walked to the bar where a tall, well built woman stood. She would have been damned pretty, as well, if her nose hadn't been larger than the rest of her features. Still, they'd been riding the trail for some time and he felt something stir inside of him. She was probably a pro, though, so he made no move to approach her.

"Beer," he told the bartender.

"Sure."

A big man with solid forearms covered with wiry, black hair, the bartender drew him a beer and set it down.

"Draw one for my friend, too, will you? He's just testing your dealer."

"Ha," the man said, "I hope you got money to pay for the drinks, because when he comes over to the bar he's gonna be broke."

"I doubt it."

"Want to make a wager?"

Clint looked at the man and said, "You're that sure of your dealer?"

"Doc's the best."

Clint knew that Wyatt was a pretty fair faro dealer himself but, not knowing how much money his friend had on him, he declined to bet.

"He said he was only going to play a couple of hands and that's not worth the bet. Another time, maybe."

"Sure," the bartender said, setting the second beer on the bar top, "any time."

As the bartender walked away the woman turned and said, "You were smart not to bet."

"You acquainted with the dealer?"

She smiled and said, "You might say that," and Clint knew what she meant.

"Is he as good as the bartender thinks he is?"

"The bartender's Mike O'Brien," she said. "He owns the place. I'm Kate Elder."

"Clint Adams."

"What's your friend's name?"

"Wyatt Earp."

Clint watched her closely to see if either name meant anything to her, but if they did it didn't show on her face.

"To answer your question, Mr. Adams, the dealer is a damn sight better than even Mike thinks."

"Guess I saved myself some money, then."

"Maybe. Gonna be in town long?"

"A few days, maybe."

"Then maybe we'll get a chance to find out."

"I'll look forward to it."

She turned and went back to what she was doing, which, Clint now realized, was watching the dealer. She had been merely friendly to Clint, not flirtatious, and he accepted that. Except for an admiring glance once in a while, he kept his distance.

Wyatt came over after about twenty minutes, looking unhappy.

"He didn't break you, did he?" Clint asked.

"No, I wasn't there long enough," Wyatt said, picking up his beer with a scowl. "It's warm."

"You said a few hands."

Clint called O'Brien over and ordered two more beers.

"That one warm?" O'Brien asked Wyatt.

"Yeah."

"I'll replace it for free."

"That's nice of you," Wyatt said.

"It was my dealer who kept you away from it, wasn't it?" the man asked.

"Yeah, I guess it was. He's pretty good."

"I told you," O'Brien said to Clint, and walked away.

"What was that about?"

"Oh, his name's O'Brien. He owns this place and wanted to bet me that the dealer would break you. The lady here backed him up."

Wyatt looked at Kate Elder with some interest and Clint said, "Forget it. She and the dealer are together."

"Did you take the bet?"

"No."

Wyatt looked insulted and said, "Why not?"

Diplomatically, Clint said, "Because your mind is not on faro."

Somewhat mollified Wyatt sipped his beer and looked over at the dealer.

"He's good."

"These people still want to bet," Clint said. "I told them maybe another time."

"Definitely another time, when I got less on my mind."

"Speaking of which, how much did Rudabaugh get from that train robbery?"

"Forty thousand."

Clint paused and then said, "You didn't tell me that in Northfield."

"Didn't tell you what?" Wyatt said, looking at Clint sharply.

"You didn't tell me that Rudabaugh got forty thousand dollars."

"I didn't?"

"No."

Wyatt scratched his head and said, "Must have slipped my mind."

"Uh-huh. Ever careful, huh, Wyatt? Even with old friends like me?"

"Keeps me in practice."

"And alive."

"That, too." Wyatt pointed his finger at the Gunsmith. "You taught me that, remember?"

"Yeah, I guess I did."

"Another beer?"

"Why not?"

"And then we'll take a little stroll around the Flat and see just what kind of a pisshole we've landed in."

Chapter Five

After Clint and Wyatt left the saloon Big Nose Kate went over to Doc Holliday and watched him deal a hand from close up. When he completed that deal she said, "Time for a break, Doc?"

Holliday looked up at her and was about to say no when he saw the look in her eyes.

Big Nose Kate didn't often look scared.

"I'll see you at the bar."

"All right, Doc."

She went back to the bar while Doc got a relief dealer, and then came over to stand next to her. Up close he could really see the fear in her eyes.

"What's wrong?"

"Two strangers were just here."

"I know," Holliday said. "I took some money from one of them."

"Well, they're not such strangers, Doc. The one you took money from was Wyatt Earp!" She gripped his arm, squeezing it urgently.

"Is that a fact?" he replied, interested.

"And the other one? He said his name was Clint Adams. That's the Gunsmith, ain't it, Doc?"

"It surely is," Holliday said, even more interested

now. "Hey, Mike, bring me a drink, will you?"

"Sure thing, Doc."

"Doc—"

"Take it easy, Kate."

"What if they're here for you?"

"Why would they be? There's no price on my head anymore, Kate."

"But . . . you're Doc Holliday."

"And they don't have any need to enhance their reputations by killing me. I don't think there's anything to worry about, Kate."

"No?"

"No," he said, accepting his drink from O'Brien. "Except, of course, for the man they *are* after."

During their circuit of the town they sidestepped two fist fights, one gun battle, and watched a potential lynching turn into a party when the potential lynch*ee* offered to buy a round of drinks for the lynch*ers*.

"Time for a drink," Wyatt finally said.

"And something to eat."

"Right."

On the way to find a decent restaurant—Wyatt laughed at the word "decent" being used to describe anything in a place like the Flat—Clint said, "So what about his faro dealer?"

"What about him?"

"Can you beat him?"

"Of course I can."

"I don't know. Those people in the saloon are pretty high on him."

"You didn't happen to get his name, by any chance, did you?"

"Uh, no, but the woman—Kate Elder—she called him Doc."

"Doc? What kind of name—wait a minute!" Wyatt said, grabbing Clint's arm and pulling him to a stop. "Did you say Doc?"

"That's what she said."

"Did you notice his cough?"

"Come to think of it, I did. Sounded worse than a cold, though. It sounded like—"

"Consumption."

"Yes. Hey, you don't think—"

"I do," Wyatt said, "I do think, Clint."

"So do I, now that you mention it."

There was no need for either of them to voice their thoughts. They were both thinking the same thing. The faro dealer was Doc Holliday!

Men of reputation invariably hear of other men of reputation, even if the reps are not as far reaching as their own. Both Clint and Wyatt had heard of Doc Holliday, and they were sure he'd heard of them.

"This could be a problem," Clint said.

"How so?"

"Well, if Holliday recognized us he might think we're here after him."

"You have a point, there."

"Or, if he'd like to build his rep a little more, he might come after one or both of us."

"Keep talking."

"That we head anything like that off as soon as we can. If we have to deal with Rudabaugh, we don't need Doc Holliday breathing down our necks."

"What are you suggesting? That one of us call Holliday out and get it over with?"

"Jesus, no! I suggest we go and talk to the man, find out if he's interested in trying one of us, and letting him know that we're not interested in him."

"Makes sense, I guess."

"And nobody gets hurt that way."

"All right, then," Wyatt said. "After we have some dinner we'll go over to the saloon and have a talk with him."

"Fine."

"I only hope he doesn't start shooting first," Wyatt said. "I don't want to have to kill him before I teach him how to play faro."

"I hope you don't want to kill him at all, Wyatt," Clint said, hoping that Wyatt Earp had not changed *that* much since they'd last seen each other.

"Of course, that's what I meant."

Chapter Six

They hadn't been able to find a good meal in town, but they'd made do with what they did find, and figured that some good whiskey would prevent any disastrous after effects.

That is, if they could find any good whiskey.

They went back to the saloon where Doc Holliday was dealing faro and as they entered the bartender, Kate Elder and Holliday were in the same positions they'd been in before. The difference was that the place was wall-to-wall people now but that didn't prevent both Kate and Holliday from spotting them as soon as they walked in.

"We've been spotted," Wyatt said.

"I know. Let's start at the bar."

"Right."

They walked to the bar and by sheer force of their presence expanded room for one into room for two. They ordered whiskey from O'Brien, who served it to them without a word.

"O'Brien," Clint said as the man started to walk away, "we'd like to talk to Doc."

O'Brien stopped and stared at them.

"You after him?"

"No, and we'd like to make sure he's not after us. We don't need that kind of trouble."

"Talk to Kate, then," O'Brien said, and walked away. They noticed that he stopped by Kate Elder, said a few words, and then she turned and located them before coming down the bar. She pushed her way in to stand next to Clint and when the man she pushed saw who she was—Doc Holliday's consort —he didn't protest.

"I hear you want to talk to Doc."

"That's right."

"What about?"

"We'd like to set down some rules," Wyatt Earp said before Clint could reply. It wasn't quite the way Clint would have put it.

"Doc doesn't like rules."

"Don't play tough for him, Kate," Clint said. "We're not after him and we hope he's not after us. We'd just like to get that straight."

"Why—"

"Just tell him that we want to talk to him. He'll talk to us."

"I just—"

"Stop trying to protect him. He doesn't need it, and I don't think he'd like it."

From the look in her eyes he knew that he was right. She hesitated just long enough to show her defiance, then left them and walked over to Doc.

After a few exchanges she returned and said, "Doc says to take a table and he'll be with you when he finishes his shift."

Clint surveyed the room and said, "There doesn't seem to be a table available."

"There is, in the back. It's Doc's table."

"Are you coming?"

"No," she said, and Clint could see that she wasn't happy about it.

"All right. Let us get a bottle—"

"I'll bring it over to you."

Clint had the notion that she wouldn't bring it over until Doc was with them in an attempt to overhear something, and he wanted it sooner than that.

"That's all right," he said, signalling for the bartender to come over. "We'd like a bottle, O'Brien."

O'Brien brought one over and said, "Here, and if you're gonna drink here you can call me Mike."

"All right, Mike. Thanks. Wyatt?"

"Yeah?"

Clint took the bottle off the bar and said, "Pay the man for the bottle."

Clint walked across the crowded room and soon spotted the empty table against the back of the wall, in a corner so that two men would be able to sit with their backs against the wall. The third was going to have to shift his chair around to see the room. Clint thought that he and Wyatt and Bat Masterson and Bill Tilghman and Doc Holliday and Luke Short and some others would look funny trying to play poker at a table when they were all trying to sit so they could see the rest of the room.

"What's so funny?" Wyatt asked when he caught up.

"Just a thought," Clint said. "Sit there, I'll shift this chair around."

"Age before beauty," Wyatt said. "You take the corner."

"Thanks."

They sat and poured drinks, then poured some

more and when they had reached the bottom of the bottle Wyatt said, "You don't suppose he's hoping we'll be drunk by the time he gets here, do you?"

At that point Mike O'Brien showed up with a fresh bottle and an extra glass. He placed the bottle in the center of the table and said, "This one's on Doc."

As the bartender walked away Clint said to Wyatt, "You might have a point."

True to his word when Holliday finished his shift he came over to the table. When he got there he stared for a moment at the unopened bottle of whiskey, then sat down.

Taking the bottle and opening it he asked, "You fellas not drinking?"

"You're the host, Doc," Clint replied. "We were waiting for you."

Holliday looked at them and Clint thought he caught a fleeting grin, perhaps a sign of respect.

"Drinking now?"

"You pouring?"

"I'm pouring."

"Then we're drinking," Clint said, and he and Wyatt extended their glasses.

Holliday dutifully poured out four drinks and then very deliberately took a sip from his, as if to say, "See, it's fine." The look on his face immediately following that added, "It's not good, but it's fine."

Clint and Wyatt tossed theirs back and Wyatt poured two more.

Clint was struck by the similarities between Holliday and Wyatt Earp. Both men were blond—though Holliday much fairer—both men wore leonine mustaches and wore them handsomely, and both men had reputations with their guns. The difference between the two men amounted to the almost half a foot in height and what might have been about forty pounds in extra weight that Wyatt was carrying around. Clint guessed that Holiday was about four or five years younger than Wyatt, which would make him about twenty-five.

"I understand you fellas want to talk to me about something."

"Well, we wanted to introduce ourselves—" Clint started, but Doc cut him off.

"There's no need for that. I know who you are."

"Well, Doc—can I call you Doc?" Clint asked.

"Why not?"

"Well, Doc, it occurred to us that you might misunderstand our presence here."

"What's not to understand. You came for the fine food, the excellent women and the good company." Holliday raised his glass as if in a toast, tossed off the contents and immediately exploded into a coughing fit that both Clint and Wyatt knew had nothing to do with the whiskey.

They waited patiently while Doc fought valiantly for control, and when the coughing had subsided it was clear that he had not won the fight, but had merely been granted a brief respite.

"Explain it to me, then," he said when he was able to speak, and Clint uncomfortably felt that he could hear death rattling about in the man's throat.

"We're here looking for a man, and not for any reason connected with you."

"Are either of you carrying a star?"

"No," Wyatt said. "I'm working for the railroad, though, tracking down a man who robbed a Sante Fe train."

"I see. What made you think I might think you were here for me?"

"Men like us," Clint said, indicating the three of them, "tend to get a little jumpy when they see . . . men like us ride into town. You start to wonder—"

"I know what you mean," Doc said. "I admit to wondering that way myself, once or twice."

"And now," Wyatt said, "it's us who are wondering."

"About me?"

Wyatt nodded.

"No need to worry about me, gents. I'm just here to deal faro."

"Not dodging any paper?" Wyatt asked.

"There are no posters on me—not anymore."

"Then we can all put our minds at ease and get on with what we're're doing," Clint said.

"As far as I'm concerned," Holliday said. He looked at Wyatt then and said, "I understand that you're a pretty fair faro player."

"I've heard the same about you."

"When you've finished your job and are able to concentrate, we should play again."

"I'll look forward to it."

"It's time for me to go back," Holliday said. "Why don't you gents stay and finish the bottle?"

"We have to be going," Clint said.

Holliday shrugged and stood up. He took one step, then turned and looked at them.

"What's the name of the man you *are* looking for?"

"Rudabaugh, Dave Rudabaugh," Wyatt said.

Clint watched Holliday's face and thought he saw a flicker of recognition.

"Do you know him?"

"I may have heard the name," Holliday said. "If I hear of anything that I think might help you, I'll let you know."

"We'd appreciate it."

A tight grin touched Holliday's mouth and he said, "Men like us have to stick together."

Clint and Wyatt went to one of the Flat's other saloons for beer and conversation. They deliberately picked one with a minimum of activity and noise, one without gaming tables of any kind, and no music.

"What do you think?" Wyatt asked.

"About Holliday?"

"No, about the weather."

"Don't get testy with me just because you don't think you can beat him at faro."

"That's a laugh! I can beat him—"

"I don't think he's looking for any trouble," Clint said, cutting off his friend's protests. "He seems to want to be left alone to play faro and do whatever else it is he's doing in this town."

"I wonder what he is doing in this town."

"A man with his rep? Maybe he's gotten smart and is just trying to keep a low profile."

"I agree—but I also think he recognized Rudabaugh's name."

"Yes, so do I."

"Should we ask him about it?"

"Maybe later. If he and Rudabaugh are friends I don't want to push him into anything."

"If he's friends with Rudabaugh he'll tell him that we're here."

"I don't think it matters who tells him, Rudabaugh's going to know we're here. It's unavoidable, given the questions we've asked. It could even be someone from the fort who tells him."

"Don't let Grant hear you say that."

After a moment Clint said, "If he is friends with Rudabaugh then he was lying to us. We might end up having to face him."

"I wonder how good he really is?"

"I hope we don't have to find out."

"I don't think he was lying."

"What makes you say that?"

"I don't know. Instinct, maybe? Maybe it's because he's like us."

"If he's holed up in this town trying to avoid trouble, then he's a lot smarter than us."

Was Wyatt Earp old enough to understand that statement, Clint wondered? Had he been through enough to know what Clint meant?

"I think we'd better turn in and be on the alert," Clint said when Wyatt didn't reply to the remark. "'Somebody might try something tonight."

"Want to move into the same room?"

Clint thought a moment and then said, "No, I don't think that's necessary. Let's keep some space between us just in case somebody simply wants to get in touch with one of us."

"Why one?"

"I'm just here backing you up," Clint said, reminding him. "Somebody might want to make a deal with the railroad through you. I don't want to scare them away."

"You have a point there. All right, let's get back to the hotel, then."

They finished their beers, left the saloon and started for their hotel, both of them acutely aware of their surroundings.

"You know," Clint said, "given the kind of place the Flat is, somebody could take a shot at us now and it could have nothing to do with Rudabaugh."

Wyatt looked at him and said, "That's a comforting thought to sleep on."

Chapter Seven

When the last customer left the Griffin Saloon Mike O'Brien locked the front door and turned to see Doc Holliday putting the faro table in order. Off to the side Kate Elder waited patiently for her man to be ready to go home.

"How about one to make sleeping easier, Mike?" Doc Holliday called.

"You got to, Doc."

O'Brien went behind the bar and poured a drink for Doc Holliday.

"Have one with me, Mike," Doc said, approaching the bar and picking up the drink.

O'Brien didn't want a drink, but he was too frightened of Doc to refuse.

"Sure, Doc."

O'Brien poured another drink and picked it up.

"Down the hatch," Doc said.

O'Brien raised his glass to Doc, then opened his mouth and poured it in.

"You know Dave Rudabaugh, don't you, Mike?"

O'Brien choked on the whiskey, bringing both hands to his mouth to catch the liquid on its way out.

Some of it ran up into his nose, making his eyes redden and tear.

"Easy, Mike, take it easy," Doc said, sipping his own whiskey.

O'Brien sputtered and choked, perhaps longer than he had to.

"You want another drink, Mike?" Doc asked when the man finally stopped coughing.

"No, thanks, Doc . . ." he gasped.

"What happened."

O'Brien shook his head and said, "Just went down . . . the wrong way . . . I guess."

"Must've," Doc said, finishing his own. "It's good whiskey."

"The best, Doc."

"You do know Dave Rudabaugh, don't you, Mike?"

"What makes you ask that?"

"Seems to me I might have heard you mention him once or twice."

"Yeah—well, yeah, I know him. Why?"

Doc shrugged and said, "Just thought I'd ask, that's all. 'Night, Mike."

"Good night, Doc."

Mike watched as Holliday collected Kate Elder, and then he let the two of them out, bidding them both good night for a last time. As soon as he had the doors secured he went back to the bar, poured himself another drink and drank it down, his hand shaking.

It was hell for a man to be afraid all the time. He just hoped that he wouldn't have to try and decide who he was more afraid of, Dave Rudabaugh or Doc Holliday.

• • •

"Why were you asking Mike about Dave Ruda-baugh, Doc?" Kate Elder asked as they walked to the three-room house they shared. Actually, it wasn't much of a house, but it had four walls and a roof and was the only wooden structure in the town that wasn't a business of some kind. Most of the "residences" in the Flat were tents.

"Just curious."

Actually, Doc didn't know why he had asked Mike the question. At least he wasn't sure. There was something about Wyatt Earp that he liked and he wasn't quite sure what or why. He respected the man, too, almost as much as he respected the legend of the Gunsmith, but although the Gunsmith was certainly the most respected shootist in the West since the demise of Hickok, Earp was closer to Doc's own age, and for that reason he felt a sort of kinship with the man.

He wasn't quite sure whether he was willing to help, taking a hand in a game that wasn't his, but if he chose to do so he wanted to have the ammunition to do it with.

"You're not thinking of getting involved, are you, Doc?" Kate Elder asked.

"In what, Katie?"

"In whatever Wyatt Earp and Clint Adams are here to do. You don't need that kind of trouble, Doc."

"I'm not looking for any trouble, Katie, believe me."

"Then what?"

"Nothing, really—"

"Are they looking for this Rudabaugh? O'Brien's

friend? Are you gonna help them?"

"Why should I help them? I don't even know them!"

"Sure you do, Doc. You know them, because you're just like them."

"Am I?"

"Sure you are. They're not smart enough to put their guns away and live normal lives, and neither are you."

"Well, I can't speak for them, Katie—" Holliday started to say as they reached the door of the house, but he was cut off mid-sentence by a coughing fit which doubled him over. Katie Elder caught him around the waist to support him and held him that way until the spasms subsided.

His voice was raspy as he said, "The've got time to live normal lives, Katie, where I don't."

"Doc, I didn't mean—"

"Forget it, Katie," Holliday said, breathing heavily. "Let's go inside and forget it."

Dave Rudabaugh looked up as the man opened the cabin door and entered. Rudabaugh turned up the lamp and the man stopped short, staring down the barrel of Rudabaugh's gun.

"Hey—"

"What are you doing here?"

"I ain't got good news, Dave," Mike O'Brien said, nervously.

"What about?"

"A couple of men who came looking for you."

"Who?"

"One of them's Wyatt Earp—"

"Earp?"

"—and the other one is Clint Adams."

"The Gunsmith!" Rudabaugh said, and even in the semi-darkness the nervous man could see the other's eyes glittering. "Looks like I made the big time, huh?"

"What?"

"Forget it. I want some whiskey, something to eat . . . and a woman."

"I can't bring a woman here—"

"Try your best to get me everything I want, Mike, huh?" Rudabaugh said, gesturing with his gun.

The man nodded jerkily, his eyes glued to the gun in Rudabaugh's hand.

"It'll have to be tomorrow, though. Is that okay?"

Rudabaugh gestured with the gun and again said, "Get out."

Mike O'Brien left, grateful to have gotten out alive. He was hiding Dave Rudabaugh because they had ridden together some years earlier, and because he was afraid of the man. He guessed, though, that he must have been more afraid of Doc Holliday, because he hadn't mentioned to Rudabaugh that Holliday had asked about him.

Maybe he would though—and maybe he'd tell Doc where Rudabaugh was. Maybe, if Mike O'Brien was lucky, they'd kill each other.

After O'Brien left, Rudabaugh holstered his gun. He was in a small shack at the far end of the Flat's red line district which, in a red line town like the Flat, was already considerably tougher than most towns.

His accommodations weren't exactly what he'd had in mind when he came here and looked up his "friend." It sure wasn't the kind of place he thought he'd be staying when he had forty thousand dollars in his saddlebags.

Wyatt Earp and the Gunsmith! Rather than being frightened by such legendary names, Rudabaugh was excited that two such men would be coming after him. God, if he managed to elude them or—better yet—kill one or both of them, he'd be made for life!

He sat back, aware of the huge erection that was filling his pants. He was horny, but he was also excited, and the combination of the two was more than he could take.

He went out to find a woman.

Chapter Eight

Sam Jessup knew that being a lawman in the Flat was not an enviable job. He'd been a lawman in other towns over his forty-three years, but being sheriff here was entirely different. For one thing, you couldn't go around locking up everybody who got drunk and started a ruckus, because there weren't enough cells for that.

So certain allowances had to be made, but there was still one thing he refused to make allowances for—murder.

The girl had been methodically beaten to death, pure and simple. He didn't have to be a detective—or a doctor—to know that. When the town doctor, Doctor Gilman, flipped her over onto her back he saw that her face was a mass of red pulp, her breasts were covered with bite and scratch marks, and there were bite marks on her thighs.

"Somebody either got very mad at her," Gilman said, "or simply went very mad."

"Is that your professional opinion, Doc?"

"An observation, Sam," Gilman said, standing up and brushing off his pants. They were inside, but the crib had no floor other than the hardpacked dirt of the street it stood on.

Doc Gilman was a small, wiry man in his sixties, dwarfed by the larger, younger lawman. His face was a mass of wrinkles and his hair white as a sheet, but his eyes were a lively blue and the wrinkes at the corners had a different cause than the other wrinkles on his face. Doc Gilman was a squinter, and had been all his life. While most people squinted against the glare of the sun, Doc Gilman squinted all of the time, and had had those wrinkles at the corners of his eyes since he was thirty. It was right about that time that he decided to stop trying to fight it, or explain it, and decided just to live with it. The wizened little physician was probably Jessup's only real friend in town.

"My professional opinion," he said, turning to face Sam Jessup with his black bag in his hand, "is that this young woman is dead."

"Well, thanks, Doc. I really needed that little piece of news. Thanks for all your help."

"I'll have her moved to the undertaker's," Gilman said, ignoring the sarcasm, "with your permission, Sheriff."

"Fine."

"And then I'll buy you a drink at the saloon."

"That'll be fine, too, Doc, but later this afternoon. I'm still not taking rotgut for breakfast."

"Gets your blood flowing," Gilman said, "but suit yourself."

The doc had some men come in, wrap the girl in the dirty sheet from her cheap bed and carry her out that way. Her blood soaked through the sheet and left little dots of red in her wake.

She'd been discovered in her Walker Street crib, in

the Northern end of town, by the man she worked for. George Talbot had many girls set up in cribs like this all over town, and he stopped in on all of them every morning to collect his money, which represented at least eighty percent of what the girls made.

Talbot looked like a well-dressed, slick-haired weasel, and right now he was sweating. Jessup had seen to the body's removal and now he and Talbot stood outside the crib, which had been fashioned from plywood and cardboard.

"Tell me about it, Talbot," Jessup said.

"About what?"

"What happened?"

"How the hell do I know. I came by to see her and she's dead. I sent for you right away, Sheriff, don't that get me any points?"

"Talbot, you could become a saint and still make no points with me."

"That ain't fair—"

"Don't talk to me about fair, you maggot. Have you seen your other girls today?"

"Yeah."

"Are they all in one piece?"

"Yeah."

"Any of them see this girl—what was her name?"

"Margaret, Mary, she used both."

"Any of them see Mary last night?"

"I dunno."

"Well ask them!" Jessup snapped. "When you've talked to all of them come and see me in my office and tell me what they said."

"You want me to do your work for you?"

Jessup backhanded Talbot across the face. The lawman was a big man with large biceps and shoulders, and Talbot's head snapped back, causing the man to see stars for a few moments. Jessup had not struck as hard as he could have, and Talbot remained standing, though somewhat unsteadily.

"Does that answer your question?"

"Sure Sheriff, sure, you don't have to get mad. Shit, I'm the one losing money, here. Mary was one of my best girls."

"You mean she carried the least diseases?"

"Aw Sheriff, you know my girls are clean."

"There's nothing clean in this town, Talbot, least of all you and your girls. Get lost now before I figure you beat her up yourself when she wouldn't come across with the money."

There was no question of that, of course, because the man's hands were unmarked. You couldn't administer a beating of this caliber without sustaining some damage to your hands—unless the man had worn gloves, but in addition to that, Talbot was a coward. Oh, he'd hit his girls from time to time, but he didn't have the stomach for a beating like this.

Not many men did, but then this was the Flat. This was the place where men like that congregated, and Jessup didn't hold out much hope of finding the guilty man.

That didn't mean he wouldn't look, though.

Chapter Nine

The night had passed uneventfully, and over breakfast Clint and Wyatt had decided to check in with the local lawman.

"If this town has one."

"It'll have one," Clint said, "even if just for the sake of appearances."

They found their way to the Sheriff's office but it was empty. There was a cup of coffee on the desk that, when Clint cupped his hand around it, still held some warmth.

"He might just have been called out. Why don't we wait?"

"Why not?"

It wasn't a long wait and soon the Sheriff entered and stopped short when he saw that he had company. He tensed, closed the door and turned to face them, an able-looking man.

"Good morning, Sheriff," Clint said, hoping to put the man at ease.

"You wouldn't think so," the man said, "not if you'd been where I just came from."

"A bad one?" Clint asked.

The lawman crossed to his desk, picked up his coffee cup, sipped and pulled a face. He crossed to his stove and warmed the coffee from the pot.

"Coffee?" he asked.

"No, thanks," Clint said, and Wyatt shook his head and stepped forward.

"Sheriff, my name's Wyatt Earp."

The sheriff's hand stopped for a scant second and then continued to lift the cup to his lips.

"I've heard of you."

"This is Clint Adams."

Now the sheriff frowned and said, "I've heard of you, too. What are you both doing in the Flat?"

"Looking for a man."

"There are a lot of them here," the man said, seating himself.

"Sheriff—"

"Jessup, Sam Jessup."

Clint looked closely at the man and said, "I've heard of you."

The man looked genuinely surprised and not a little pleased.

"You have?"

"You cleaned out a town called Twin Forks, in Kansas—oh, what? Ten years ago?"

"Closer to fifteen," Jessup said. "I was a lot younger then."

"We all were," Clint said, not bothering to look at Wyatt, who would have been all of fourteen then.

"I didn't do much after that, I'm afraid," Jessup said. "I thought I would, after that, you know? But . . ."

"I know," Clint said. "You tracked down Dan Maitland, though—"

"Dan Maitland!" Jessup said, staring at something only he could see. "Jesus, that was eight—nine years ago."

"You didn't do too badly," Clint said. "Your name's respected—"

"And look where I ended up," Jessup said, spreading his hands to indicate his present domain. "What can I do for you fellas?"

"I'm working for the railroad, looking for a man named Rudabaugh."

"Never heard of him."

Clint felt the man was telling the truth.

"We want you to know we're here," Clint said, "and although we're looking for Rudabaugh, we're not looking for trouble."

"You know Doc Holliday's here, don't you?"

"We've already talked to Doc."

"Well . . . good."

"I guess that's all," Clint said. "You've obviously got something on your mind, so we'll leave you alone."

As Clint and Wyatt started for the door Jessup called out, "Adams."

"Yeah?"

"Maybe while you're in town we could . . . have a drink, sometime."

Clint grinned and said, "Talk about old times?"

"Why not?"

"Sure," Clint said, "why not?"

"Sam Jessup," Clint said as they stepped outside.

"I never heard of him."

"You wouldn't have. He's one of those people you always wonder what happened to."

"Was he any good?"

"He was very good." Clint was puzzled. How had Jessup come to end up here?

"How did he end up here?" Wyatt asked, voicing Clint's own unspoken question.

"Damned if I know. Maybe I'll find out over a drink or two."

"Can we count on him?"

Clint hesitated and then said, "I guess I'll have to find that out, too."

Inside Sam Jessup drank his coffee without tasting it, thinking first about the past, and then about the present and, finally, the future.

The past he thought about was his own, and he hadn't thought about it in a long time. The presence of one of his contemporaries, Clint Adams, the famous Gunsmith, started him thinking again of the things he'd done right, the things he'd done wrong. The latter certainly outnumbered the former, his presence here was testimony to that.

The present he thought about involved the murder of the whore, and the presence of two known gunmen—three if you counted Holliday—in his town. That never boded well, but at least none of them had a reputation for wanton killing.

His own future was something else he rarely contemplated, but he thought about it now. Having Clint Adams in town was perhaps something he should not allow to simply go by. The man had obviously done more right in his life than wrong. His rep was testimony to *that* fact, even if he didn't think so himself.

At the very least things stood to get pretty interesting.

* * *

When Dave Rudabaugh awoke the next morning he ran his right hand over his face, rubbing his eyes with thumb and forefinger, trying to remember what had happened last night. He'd found a woman, he knew that much, and she had a bottle of whiskey.

He leaned on his left hand and gasped in pain. Holding it up he saw that it was bruised and swollen, and the skin was cracked over the center knuckle.

Jesus, he thought, at least he hadn't been drunk enough to use his gun hand.

Chapter Ten

Sitting over a couple of noon beers Clint and Wyatt decided to attack the situation head on instead of trying to be subtle.

"Subtlety was never my strong point, anyway," Wyatt reasoned.

"Mine, either."

"Maybe the bastard will come after us. That would make our job easy."

"What's his rep?"

"I've heard he's handy with a gun."

"I doubt that he'll try to take us both at one time."

"I agree."

"That means we'll have to split up, because if we stay together he'll never come out of his hole."

"Agreed."

Clint changed his train of thought.

"Have you thought of something else, Wyatt?"

"What do you mean?"

"What if he's not here?"

"He's here," Wyatt said, firmly. "I chased him a long way, Clint, and he headed straight for here. There's nothing else around here for him."

"What if he was here and left?"

"What makes you so negative?"

"I'm not negative. I'm trying to cover all possibilities."

"All right. We'll give it a couple days here, question some people, push some of them—like our friend the bartender, there—and then if we don't find him we'll assume he either left or never stopped here."

"I thought you were firm in your belief that he did?"

"And I thought you wanted to cover all the possibilities. Are you changing your mind now?"

Chagrined, Clint said, "No, I'm not. What do we do after a couple of days?"

"Forget about it?"

"What? After you tracked him all this way? I thought you wanted him."

What Wyatt said next puzzled Clint.

"*I* don't want him, the railroad wants him. I'll go a long way to accommodate them, but I'm not fanatical about it."

"That sounds like you're tracking him only for the money they're paying you."

Wyatt stared into his beer and said, "Is that what it sounds like?"

They dropped the subject after that because they were getting too close to a discussion of values, and how they change over the years. There was a time when Wyatt Earp would have tracked a criminal simply because he *was* a criminal.

This Wyatt Earp sounded almost like a bounty hunter.

Still, whichever Wyatt Earp he was, he was still

Clint's friend, and the Gunsmith would stay and help him as long as he needed it.

"All right, we'll split up then and meet back here around sundown to compare notes," Clint said.

"And to have dinner."

"And to have dinner."

"And maybe for something else, too," Wyatt said, and Clint knew what he meant.

A woman had descended the staircase and it was plain from her demeanor and dress that she worked there. It was also plain as the nose on a hound's face that she was a beauty. Tall and slender, yet with a full bosom, she had dark hair piled high atop her head to show off a long, graceful neck.

"Where was she yesterday?" Wyatt wondered aloud.

"Maybe she was out sick."

"Maybe."

"I'm going to find out her name," Wyatt said, beginning to rise.

She spoke briefly to the bartender then turned and went back up the stairway the way she had come.

"Looks like you're going to have to wait until tonight, Romeo," Clint said.

Wyatt sat back down and said, "I don't mind. That's something worth waiting for." He looked at Clint and asked, "You're not interested too, are you?"

Clint shrugged and said, "She's probably a working girl."

"Still won't pay for it, huh?"

"Some values don't change," Clint said before he realized what he was going to say."

In a somewhat strained silence they rose and left

the saloon and then split up.

Belinda Darnell went back to her room on the second floor to change her clothes. When her boss, Mike O'Brien, had said that he had work for her she'd assumed he meant in the saloon. She'd assumed wrong. As soon as he saw her enter the room he'd called her over and told her to change her clothes. He told her that he had someone he wanted her to "entertain" outside the saloon.

O'Brien had used Belinda to entertain before, but she was starting to tire of it. She wished that she had never started in this business of being a saloon girl and part-time whore. She wished she could give her body only when she wanted to, to a man she wanted, but what else was there for her to do? How would she make a living if she quit O'Brien's saloon?

Maybe, she thought as she changed into a more simple dress that nevertheless still showed off her figure, maybe she should just quit and leave town, leave the Flat. It was a horrible place to live, anyway.

Who was she kidding? If she wanted to leave the Flat she'd have to do so on foot, because she didn't have the money for stage passage.

And that brought her full circle, because the only way she knew how to get the money was by using her body. Maybe she should leave O'Brien and set herself up. She paused in the act of dressing and looked at herself in the mirror.

She was twenty-eight, tall and slender, but she had good breasts and knew it. They were high and firm and actually looked larger than they really were. She cupped them in her hands and squeezed lightly to reaffirm that they were still in that conditon and had not started to sag or soften. It happened, she knew, to some women as they approached thirty.

Her nipples were brown, dark brown, and the aureola were unusually large so that her breasts seemed to be almost all nipple. She had never had a problem pleasing men either with the way she looked or performed, but the problem in setting herself up was the old one: money.

She could have gotten herself a crib at the north end of town but then she'd be working for Talbot, and you only did that when you were *really* desperate.

She turned away from the mirror and continued to get dressed.

No, for now it seemed that she was stuck right where she was, working for O'Brien and occasionally servicing one of his friends or special clients.

She wondered which one it would be this time.

When she got downstairs she went over to O'Brien so he could tell her where to go. He started to give her directions but she stopped him abruptly when she realized where he was sending her.

"Wait a minute, Mike."

"What's the matter?"

"I'm not working the cribs."

"No, of course you're not working the cribs, but my friend, he's holed up in one of the cribs. That's where you have to meet him."

Belinda frowned.

"Is this another one of your friends who's on the run from the law?"

"Yes, and don't mention that to him or he'll get mad. He's got a lot of money, Belinda, and if you handle it right he could give some of it to you."

"How much is a lot?"

"An awful lot, Belinda—" he started to say but then thought better of it. "But never mind that. Just go over there and . . . please him."

"All right," she said, thinking of the money. "Tell me where it is, again."

He gave her the directions again.

Chapter Eleven

Before Clint realized it he had crossed over the mythical red line—although how a town like the Flat could have a red line he didn't know. It looked pretty much the same to him as the rest of the town.

Curious to see if it would change he kept walking, and eventually he came to the cribs. They were falling down, one-room shacks built of plywood and cardboard and how any man could pay to go in there with a woman and satisfy his sexual urges was beyond him—but then never having had the urge to pay for his pleasures, perhaps he was judging too harshly. Maybe that was the only way some men *could* get satisfaction.

Disgusted with his surroundings he turned to leave when he spotted the same woman he and Wyatt had seen in the saloon earlier, and paused to watch her.

She was picking her way through the cribs as if she were looking for one in particular.

Surely she couldn't be working here . . .

Even the smell of the cribs disgusted Belinda Darnell, and practically banished all the thoughts she'd had about going out on her own. God, if there was even the slightest chance that she could end up here . . .

Intent on finding the crib O'Brien had described, she didn't see the man come up on her until it was too late. He had her by the arm before she knew what was happening.

"Hey little lady, which one of these little pleasure palaces is yours, huh?"

"Let go of me!" she snapped.

The man was filthy and huge, a monster of a man swathed from head to toe in what looked like greasy rags. He leaned over so that his face was near hers and she could smell his fetid breath.

"Now, don't get shy on me, girlie. I got money to pay you, and a big cock to give you a good time. Whataya say?"

She was reacting badly, she knew, but she was frightened and shouted at him.

"Let go, you revolting animal!"

The man frowned, as if trying to understand her words, and if he didn't he certainly caught her tone.

"Who you callin' a animal?" he demanded. "You want to see an animal? I'll show you an animal."

She didn't know how he had done it but with one hand still holding onto her wrist he managed to expose himself using the other. His cock was huge and thickly veined and the smell that came from his crotch made her gag.

"See what I got for you, girlie? That change your mind, huh?"

She looked around frantically, wondering if there was any help for her, but everyone seemed occupied with their own business.

"Damn you!" she yelled angrily, and she kicked

him in the shin as hard as she could.

"Bitch!" he snapped, slapping her across the face hard with the back of his free hand.

Clint knew he had waited too long, but there had been the slight chance that the man was a customer. Now as he saw her fall and moved forward he was ashamed that he hadn't known better. Whatever she was here for, she certainly wasn't working the cribs.

As he got nearer them he heard the big man yell, "Bitch!" and lift a huge foot to stomp her. He knew he could have shot but he disdained his gun and threw himself at the man, striking him at the knees and taking his legs out from under him. The man had been reaching for the woman again and had his hand on her dress as he was hit. Clint heard something tear as they both went down hard.

Clint was the first to get to his feet. He moved so that he would be standing between the woman and the big man and waited for the man to rise.

"Please," the woman said behind him.

"Stay there," he warned her.

The man got to his feet and walked over to face Clint.

"What'd you do that for?"

"I don't think the lady appreciates your proposition, friend. Why don't you tuck yourself in and be on your way?"

"I can't tuck this in until I get it taken care of," the man complained, indicating what was now a huge, obscene erection.

"Get it taken care of somewhere else. This lady is not available."

"You claimin' her?"

Thinking that was his way out Clint said, "That's right, I'm claimin' her."

The man grinned then, exposing a yellow, gap-toothed smile and said, "You got to fight for her, then. I'll stomp *you*. Stompin' is almost as good as fuckin', anyway."

The man began to move forward and Clint threw a hard right into his face. The man's head rocked back, he kept coming and hit Clint with his entire forearm, sweeping him out of the way. Instead of going for Belinda however, the man turned towards Clint and lifted his foot to stomp him.

"Shoot him!" Belinda yelled. "Shoot him or he'll kill you!"

Clint hated to admit it but he thought she might be right. The man was so big and dumb that he didn't think he'd be able to hurt him. He didn't think that the word "hurt" was even in the man's limited vocabulary. Even Belinda's kick had been more of an annoyance than anything else.

Clint rolled out of the way of the huge foot and got to his feet.

"Look, friend, I don't want to have to shoot you."

The man looked at Clint's gun, and then at his face.

"You'd shoot me?"

"I'm not going to just let you stomp me. Is she worth dying for?"

That puzzled the man and he had to stop and think about it. Finally, he scratched his head and said, "You'd shoot me? I ain't got a gun."

"If I don't shoot you, you'll kill me."

"I'll just stomp you a little. How's that?"

"No good."

Now the man looked as if he wanted to cry.

"I gotta get taken care of—"

"Look," Clint said, digging into his pocket for a couple of double eagles, "there are plenty of women here. Go and find another one, huh? On me?"

The man looked insulted.

"I got my own money. I can pay."

Suddenly, Clint felt badly that he had insulted the man, and then realized how ridiculous that was.

"Look—" he said.

"Forget it," the man said, waving a big paw. "Too much trouble," and walked off.

Clint let out a breath and moved to help the woman to her feet. He took her hands and pulled her up so that she was standing next to him. She was almost as tall as he was. She made an attempt to cover herself where her dress had been torn away.

"Oh, thank you," she said brushing a stray strand of hair from her forehead. "I don't know how to—"

"You're from the saloon," he said, cutting her off. "I saw you there earlier."

"That's right," she said. "You'd think I'd have learned to handle men like that by now, but he scared me, and he was so big . . ."

In more ways than one, Clint thought she might have added.

"What are you doing in this part of town?"

"I was, uh, looking for someone," she replied, evasively.

"Well, maybe I can help you find him—"

"Forget it," she said, rubbing her cheek where the big man had hit her. Clint saw that a bruise was starting to form. "I'm going back before something else happens. Mike can find himself another—I can't be walking around like this."

She stopped abruptly and Clint figured that "Mike" must have meant O'Brien, the man who owned the saloon, and he must have sent her here to meet someone.

"I'll walk you back, if you like."

"I'd rather not go back to the saloon."

"You can change and clean up in my room, if you like."

"That would be nice," she said, immediately. "I'm just a little rattled, or I wouldn't ask you—"

"You didn't ask," he said, cutting her off, "I offered. Shall we?" He offered her his arm, she took it and they started back to the more civilized section of town.

Of course, Clint Adams didn't expect to end up in bed with Belinda Darnell, especially since Wyatt Earp had expressed an interest in her, but when they got to his room they both realized that she could have gone to her room to clean up and she certainly couldn't change clothes in his because she didn't have anything to change into.

Her breasts were firm as she pushed them into his face from her position atop him. His tongue flicked out to taste her nipples, which were as hard as pebbles, and then he began to chew on them. His penis, already imbedded deep inside her, began to be massaged in a very intriguing way by her muscles. Soon she was bouncing up and down on him, making it hard for him to maintain mouth-to-breast contact, but soon that was forgotten as the rush of orgasm carried them both over the edge.

"Do you have a needle and thread?" she asked later.

"Did you ever know a travelling man who didn't?" he asked. He produced them and then watched as she sat cross-legged and naked on his bed, trying to effect some repairs on her dress so she could wear it back to her room.

"That was wonderful, you know," she said.

"Yes, it was."

"I mean, I know you think I'm a professional at being with men—"

"I'm not asking any questions, Belinda."

"Well, I guess I am a professional, although I would prefer not to be."

"Belinda—"

"Oh, shut up. Talking's good for the soul."

So he listened while she told him her hopes and dreams of leaving the Flat and he started to wonder if she weren't hinting that he should take her with him when he left.

If she *was* hinting, he wasn't picking up on it.

"There, I think that's the best I can do. Thanks for the needle and thread."

He would have said, "Anything for a lady," but he was afraid she might leap on that as an offer to take her with him when he left.

"I guess I'd better get back to the saloon and tell Mike what happened."

"I'm sure he'll understand."

She stood up and got dressed while he watched and then leaned over to kiss him.

"Thanks for everything, Clint. The rescue, listening to me talk, and . . . well, you know."

"I know, Belinda."

"Will you be in town much longer?"

"I don't really know, Belinda."

"Well, if you are, maybe we can see each other again."

"We'll have to see what happens."

"Sure," she said. She hesitated a moment before leaving, as if she expected him to say something, then said, "Sure," again, opened the door and left.

Now that it was over he was sorry that he had taken her to bed, but it had been as much her idea as his. He expected Wyatt to bed her. He only hoped that she wasn't the type that talked about one man with another. She hadn't been with him, but then the circumstances had been different.

She was a nice kid and he hoped that she would eventually find her way out of the Flat.

It was up to Mike O'Brien to explain to Rudabaugh what had happened to the woman he'd been promised. He didn't relish the job. Hopefully, the food he was bringing him would make up for it in a small way.

The bruise on Belinda's cheek had attested to the fact that she hadn't been lying. She'd been attacked on the way to see Rudabaugh, and had been in no shape after that to continue. O'Brien, being a reasonable man, had been able to accept that.

Dave Rudabaugh, on the other hand, had never been accused of being a reasonable man.

To O'Brien's everlasting surprise Rudabaugh accepted the bag of sandwiches and, munching vigorously on two at once told him not to worry about the woman.

"I took care of that myself."

"You went out?"

"Last night. Found me a woman, got taken care of, and came back. Good sandwiches, Mike. Turkey?"

"Chicken."

"Tastes like turkey."

The enormity of Rudabaugh's statement struck O'Brien when he remembered that a woman had been killed in the cribs the night before. For a moment he almost mentioned it to Rudabaugh but caught himself.

"Something on your mind, Mike?"

"Huh? Oh no, nothing, Dave, nothing at all."

"Well, there's something on mine."

"What's that?"

"Clint Adams."

"The Gunsmith?"

"Yeah. I wanna try him."

"Dave—he's fast!" O'Brien said, not bothering to disguise the respect, the *awe*, he felt.

"And I ain't?"

Fear was not as easy to disguise.

"That ain't what I meant, Dave. Uh, what about Wyatt Earp?"

"Kill him."

"W-what?"

"Oh, I don't mean you, Mike. I know you can't kill nobody."

"Dave—"

"Have it done. I'm sure there's plenty of men in the Flat who'd kill him for twenty dollars or more."

"Why . . . like that?"

"I can't face but one of them, Mike. If I face them both one or the other might end up killing me. You wouldn't want that to happen, would you?''

"Uh, no, Dave, no.''

"I didn't think so. Besides, the Gunsmith's the one with the bigger rep. If I kill him I'll be made for life.''

"I guess . . .''

"So have Earp killed, and Mike—''

"Yeah, Dave?''

"Next time you bring me sandwiches, bring me a bottle of whiskey, too.''

"Sure, Dave,'' O'Brien said, backing out of the crib, "Sure.''

It took Mike O'Brien all of fifteen minutes—the walk back to the saloon—to make up his mind. It might cost Wyatt Earp his life, but he was fairly sure that the Gunsmith would kill Dave Rudabaugh in a fair fight, and *that* would keep Mike O'Brien alive.

Chapter Twelve

Doc Holliday left Kate Elder's house about the time Mike O'Brien was talking with four men and money was changing hands. It was a brisk morning and sometimes on mornings like this Doc felt as if he had more life left than he actually did. That is, until the coughing started . . .

Wyatt Earp was wandering about the south end of town, away from the red line, keeping a sharp eye out for any sign of Dave Rudabaugh. Even if the man was holed up he had to come out for air sometime. He also kept his ears open on the off chance that somebody might mention the man's name. After an hour or so of that he tired of being subtle and began to ask questions.

Juice Newton and his three friends had not been told who the man was they were to kill. He had simply been described to them, a tall, lean man with a flat brimmed hat, black hair and one sidearm. If Juice—named because of his proficiency with squirting tobacco juice with accuracy up to fifty feet—had had any brains, he would have wondered why it would take four men to do the job.

Then again, Juice *was* known more for squirting than he was for thinking and his friends were no smarter.

Holliday saw Wyatt Earp and the four men at the same time, before they saw each other. He stopped to watch.

"Hey!"

Wyatt heard the voice call out and knew instinctively that it was meant for him. The other people on the street knew it too, for they took one look at the tableau that was forming and deserted the streets.

Wyatt turned and looked at the four men, none of whom were Dave Rudabaugh.

"You talking to me?"

"That's right."

The speaker was a husky man, typical of the type seen in the flat—dirty, scruffy, and wearing a well worn Colt on his right hip. At that moment the man squirted an impressive stream of brown tobacco juice, striking a small mongrel dog right in the eye with it. The dog cried out and ran.

"That's real impressive. What else can you do?'

"I do what I get paid to do, mister," the man said.

"Which is?"

"To kill you."

Wyatt looked at the other three men who had fanned out so that they were standing four abreast all told.

"They getting paid, too?"

"Yep."

"You know who you're killing?"

"It don't matter."

"Who hired you?"

The man squirted again and said again, "It don't matter."

Wyatt took in all four men now, gauging them carefully. They were standing easy, confident, and had obviously done this before.

"At least let me identify myself before you kill me. I get a last request, don't I?"

The man laughed, showing teeth stained by years of chewing.

"Sure, friend. Go ahead, identify yourself."

"The name's Earp, Wyatt Earp."

Wyatt knew that if he had said that his name was Clint Adams the four of them would have recognized the name immediately. Clint was his friend and he wouldn't have minded having his name borrowed, but that just wasn't Wyatt Earp's game.

He watched the men to see if any of them would recognize the name and was satisfied to see a glint of recognition in the squirter's eyes.

"It ain't any easier when you know who you're killing, is it?"

The squirter did some fast thinking and decided that, Wyatt Earp or no, the odds were still four to one in his favor.

Deciding to brazen it out he said for a third time, "It don't matter."

"Have it your way, then."

"Mind if I buy into this game?" a new voice asked.

Wyatt waited for the squirter to look away before he did. He knew that the other three men would not make a move before their leader did. What they both saw was a slightly built blond man who moved in to stand next to Wyatt.

" 'Morning, Doc.''

"You seem to be facing heavy odds here, Wyatt.''

"Not as heavy as they look, Doc, but an extra hand is always welcome.''

"That's Doc Holliday,'' one of the three men with the squirter said.

"Shut up!'' the leader said. "It's still four guns to two.''

"You fellas want to change your plans for the day, now's the time to do it,'' Wyatt called out.

The three men exchanged glances, but they remained under the influence of the tobacco squirter.

"Have it your own way,'' Wyatt said.

The squirter spat a stream of brown juice into the dirt and then went for his gun.

The other three followed.

The squirter caught the first bullet high in the chest and died before he hit the ground.

The other three followed him there.

Wyatt and Doc holstered their weapons and went to examine the damage.

"All dead,'' Doc said.

"You were pretty fast,'' Doc said.

"So were you.''

"Any idea who these fellows were?'' Doc asked, nudging the squirter with his boot. Brown juice had leaked from the man's mouth to mingle with the red blood on his chest.

"Hired guns, Doc.''

"Working for who?''

"I got a hunch.''

"That fellow you're looking for?''

"Or somebody working with him.''

Wyatt turned to look at Doc and said, "Can I buy

you a drink, Doc? I owe you."

"Sure."

"Can we get one this early?"

"This is the Flat, Wyatt," Doc said. "You can get anything."

"Even this early?"

Doc grinned and said, "It don't matter."

Chapter Thirteen

"Adams!"

Clint turned at the sound of the voice and saw Sheriff Sam Jessup bearing down on him.

"What's wrong, Sheriff?"

"Your friend Earp and Doc Holliday just gunned down four men."

"I'm impressed."

"I'm not. Where are they?"

"I was told they were in the Griffin Saloon. I'm headed there now."

"I'll tag along. Maybe we can get that drink."

"I doubt it." Jessup said, as they headed for the saloon.

Clint had only made the suggestion to try to settle the lawman down, but he could see that the only thing that was going to do that was an explanation from Wyatt Earp and Doc Holliday about why they'd killed four men.

He was kind of interested in hearing that, himself.

Ironically, after leaving a message with a bystander about where they would be when the sheriff asked, they went to Mike O'Brien's for that drink.

O'Brien almost bolted and ran when he saw Wyatt and Holliday enter the saloon together, but he stayed put long enough to notice that neither man had any particular interest in him. They entered and went right to Holliday's table.

"Mike, two beers," Holliday called out.

"Coming up, Doc."

O'Brien took a swipe at his brow with his bar rag to remove the beads of sweat that had formed there before taking the two men their beers, and then fled back to the safety of his bar.

"Got any ideas?" Holliday asked. They were the only two customers in the place.

"About who hired those four?"

Holliday nodded.

"I don't think Rudabaugh did it himself. He's obviously holed up somewhere. In fact, this just about confirms that he's here, somewhere."

"Not necessarily," Holliday said. "He could have left these four behind to wait for you."

Wyatt shook his head.

"He didn't know I was trailing him. If he sent those four after me it's because he's in town and has heard that I'm looking for him."

"Makes sense."

"What about you?" Wyatt asked. "Any ideas about who hired them?"

"Why would I have?"

Wyatt shrugged and said, "You live here. Did you know any of them?"

"Saw them once or twice in here, at the bar."

"Any of them play your table?"

"One, the fellow with the tobacco."

"Did he seem to know anyone in here?"

Holliday shrugged.

"They talked to each other, the bartender to order drinks, and the squirter talked to me to play cards."

"Maybe the bartender can tell me something."

Holliday, remembering that the man knew Dave Rudabaugh, said, "Maybe he can."

He was not yet ready to turn his employer over to Wyatt Earp as a possible suspect. He'd talk to the man himself, first.

Wyatt was in the act of standing up when the batwing doors opened and Clint walked in, followed closely by the sheriff.

"Hello, Clint," Wyatt said, "Sheriff. Join us for a drink?"

"I'm not here for a drink, Earp," Jessup said.

"Now, Sam," Holliday said, "settle down. We've got an explanation."

"I'd like you to explain why you left the scene of the shooting without waiting for me?"

"Killing's thirsty work, Sam," Holliday said.

"That's the kind of answer I'd expect from you, Doc, but you," he said to Wyatt, "you should know better."

"You want an explanation or not, Sheriff?" Wyatt asked calmly.

"I do."

"Then stop jumping down our throats long enough for us to give you one."

Jessup tightened his lips and then said, "All right, go ahead."

Wyatt explained about being braced by the four

men and Doc stepping in to help them out. He also
told the lawman that he gave the men ample opportunity to back out.

"He's got that right, Sam, they just weren't smart
enough to take the chance that was given them."

"This have something to do with why you're here,
or do you think it was personal?" Jessup asked
Wyatt.

"Couldn't be personal, Sheriff, because I didn't
know any of those men."

"Maybe they were just after a rep."

"They said they were being paid, Sheriff."

"By who?"

"That they didn't say."

"Too bad one of them ain't still alive to tell us."

"You've killed your share of men, Jessup," Holliday said. "You know that you don't always have a
choice."

Grudgingly, Jessup said, "You're right about that.
All right, one of you will have to stop by my office
later and sign a statement."

"I'll do that, Sheriff," Wyatt said. "Now, how
about having that drink with us?"

"Not right now, thanks. I've got to see about getting the streets cleaned."

He started away and then abruptly turned back to
face them.

"I would also like them to stay clean, this time."

"You have my word, Sheriff," Wyatt said. "I
won't kill another man—as long as I have a choice."

Jessup turned, nodded at Clint, and then left.

"He used to be a hell of a good man," Clint said.

"Still is, Adams," Holliday said, "He just doesn't
have much use for me. He's also got a lot on his

mind. You fellows hear about the murder?"

"The girl?" Clint asked. He'd heard people talking about it all morning.

"I heard about it, too. What do you know about it, Doc?" Wyatt asked.

"Not much," Holliday said. "Just that a prostitute in one of the cribs was beaten to death."

"That kind of a killing," Clint said, "it could have been anybody."

"That's what he's got to deal with. What about you, Adams. You feel like a beer?"

"It's a little early," Clint said, then pulled out a chair and said, "but why the hell not?"

Chapter Fourteen

When Holliday produced a deck of cards they decided to talk over a friendly game of poker.

"How friendly?" Wyatt asked.

They decided to play for a dollar and two with a three raise limit.

"Check and raise?" Wyatt asked.

"Always," Holliday said.

So much for a friendly game.

Holliday dealt the first hand, calling draw poker, and asked Wyatt, "What are your plans now?"

Wyatt looked at his cards and said, "First I plan to open for two dollars, but I assume you mean what are we going to do about finding Dave Rudabaugh."

Clint called and so did Holliday, saying, "That's what I meant. Cards."

Wyatt took two while Clint, holding a pair of eights, took three. Holliday studied his hand for a moment, then took one card.

"Two dollars," Wyatt said.

"Raise two," Clint said.

"Let's make it six," Holliday said.

"I'll take the last raise," Wyatt said, and both men called his raise.

Wyatt spread his hand, showing his openers, three

kings. He hadn't improved on them. Clint put his cards down, showing three eights and a pair of deuces.

"Full house."

"So do I," Holliday said, "but mine's higher."

He put his cards down on the table stacked, then spread them easily, one at a time. An ace, a six, another ace, a six, and another ace.

"This could get interesting," Wyatt said. He gathered up the cards while Doc raked in his thirty dollars.

"To answer your question," Wyatt said, shuffling the cards, "I don't rightly know what to do next. I intended to push a little and see what happened, and something did."

"And nobody's left alive to talk about it," Clint said.

"You weren't there—" Holliday said.

"I'm not criticising anyone, Doc," Clint hastened to add, "just stating a fact. One of those boys could have told us who hired them. Now none of them can talk."

"Maybe the thing to do," Wyatt said, wishing to avoid an argument between the other two men, "would be to find out who those other men were friendly with and start pushing them a little."

"We pushed already and look where it got us," Clint reminded him.

"Do you have another suggestion?" Wyatt asked, dealing out the cards for a hand of five card stud. He dropped a king in front of Clint, an ace in front of Holliday and a queen in front of himself. "Ace bets."

Since there were no pairs to bet on Holliday said, "I'll say a dollar."

"Call," Wyatt said.

"I call and raise a dollar," Clint said. He had another king in the hole and a pair of them was a powerful hand as could be when you played five card stud.

"I might have an idea or two," Clint said as Wyatt dealt out their third card. Clint paired, as did Holliday, and Wyatt dropped a ten on his queen.

"Pair of aces bet," Wyatt said.

Holliday said, "I'll bet two."

"Call," Wyatt said.

"Raise," said Clint.

"Call," said Holliday, tightly. "Why not tell us your plan, Adams?"

There was something in the tone of Holliday's voice that Clint didn't like. It implied that it was Holliday and Wyatt who were the team, and Clint was the interloper.

"I think I'll discuss my plans with Wyatt in private, Doc—no offense."

Wyatt looked at Clint and said, "He pulled my bacon out of the fire, Clint."

"Begging your pardon, Wyatt, but that was your bacon, not mine. For all I know, Doc here is a friend of Dave Rudabaugh's and is pumping us for information."

Clint looked at his fourth card, which was a no-help seven. Doc had pulled a nine, and Clint had a hunch that meant something. He felt that Holliday was sitting on two pairs—aces and nines—which was a damned hard hand to beat when you were only playing with five cards—unless, of course, you had three of a kind.

"Doc?" Wyatt asked.

Doc Holliday, however, was ignoring his cards and

staring hard at Clint Adams.

"I don't like being called a liar, Adams."

"I didn't call you a liar, Doc. I'm telling my partner here that I prefer to be careful around strangers, and I'm just telling him something that could happen. It is conceivable that you could turn out to be a friend of Dave Rudabaugh's."

"Not to me, it isn't."

"Can we play this hand out?" Wyatt asked. "Doc, it's your bet."

Holliday stared at Clint a little longer, then said, "I want to raise the limit."

"Fine with me. Clint?"

"Whatever Doc wants is fine."

"I'll bet twenty," Holliday said.

"I'll fold and watch you fellas bump heads," Wyatt said, flipping his cards over and folding his arms across his chest until it was time for him to deal the fifth card.

"I'll raise you twenty, Doc," Clint said.

"And I'll raise you back."

"Call. Let's see your last card, Wyatt."

Incredibly, Wyatt dropped another king on Clint, and a third ace on the table for Holliday.

"Three aces," Wyatt said in awe. "You bet, Doc."

"Fifty dollars," Holliday said. He reached for the money and said to Clint, "Not too rich for you, is it, Adams?"

"No, Doc, it's not too rich," Clint said, "even if this did start out as a friendly game. I'm calling your fifty and raising a hundred."

Wyatt watched in fascination as the two men went around the table again and he knew there was much more going on here than just poker.

Finally, Clint said, "I'm just calling here, Doc, because I don't want to break you."

"You're crazy," Holliday said. He flipped his cards over and said, "I got a full house, aces over nines."

"Good hand . . ."

Holliday leaned forward to reap in his rewards.

". . . but not good enough."

"What?"

"Four kings, Doc, all in a row."

Holliday's eyes narrowed and he sat back in his chair, breathing hard. For a moment Clint thought he was going to have a coughing fit, but he didn't.

Clint raked in his winnings and said to Wyatt, "Listen, I'm going to go and put an idea to work. I'll let you know if it pans out."

"Fine."

Clint looked at Doc Holliday and said, "No hard feelings, Doc."

"No," Holliday said, and then added, "Not from the card game."

Chapter Fifteen

Later, Clint returned to the hotel to find Wyatt waiting for him in the lobby.

"Wyatt. Game over?"

"The game was over when you left. Let's go to your room and talk."

"Fine."

When they were in Clint's room Wyatt said, "What was the big idea?"

"I didn't raise the limit, Wyatt, he did—and you dealt the cards."

"I'm not talking about the game. You were baiting Holliday. Why?"

"I just wanted to see how he'd react."

"Do you think he's friends with Dave Rudabaugh?"

"I don't know. Do you?"

"No."

"It's a possibility, though, isn't it?"

After a moment Wyatt said, "Sure, anything's possible."

Clint spread his hands and said, "That's all I was saying. I just don't trust him as much as you do."

"He didn't have to side with me."

"You're right, he didn't."

"Doesn't that say something for him?"

"Yes."

"But you still don't trust him."

"I'm just naturally a suspicious man, Wyatt. It comes with age. Having stayed alive this long, I wouldn't mind staying alive a bit longer, and you won't by taking strangers at face value."

"Is this a lesson?"

"No lesson, Wyatt, just fact. As I see it, you like Holliday and he likes you. That's fine. I hope you stay friends for a long time."

"But—"

"But I don't think that he and I will ever be friends. Just as there's something drawing the two of you together, there's something there that will always keep him and me apart."

"What?"

Clint didn't want to say that he thought it was Wyatt himself, so he simply shrugged and said, "I don't know. Some men just don't hit it off right away."

Wyatt hesitated a moment then said, "I think he wants to help us."

"Did he say so?"

"No, but I think he knows something and he's trying to decide whether or not to tell me."

"If he agrees to help you, does that mean you won't need me anymore?"

"Hell, no," Wyatt said. "There's a possibility here that we haven't talked about, Clint."

"Which is?"

"That Rudabaugh came here to meet up with somebody."

"Or a bunch of somebodies."

"Right, in which case Doc's gun might come in handy."

"Well, I can't argue that."

"Then how about trying to get along with him?"

"I'm a lot older than he is, Wyatt," Clint said. "He should be trying to get along with me."

"Clint—"

Clint held up his hands and said, "All right, all right, I'll try."

"Good. He's invited me to have dinner with him and Kate Elder tonight."

"That's fine. I'll just nose around a bit more and see what I can scare up."

"Just be careful. They tried for me once, there might be somebody out there waiting to try for you."

Clint looked at Wyatt and said, "Kid, there's always somebody waiting out there to try for me."

O'Brien went to see Rudabaugh to tell him what had happened with Wyatt Earp.

"He's not dead?" Rudabaugh asked in disbelief. "I told you to have him killed."

"I know you did, Dave, and I tried. I hired four men to gun him down."

"And what happened?"

"Doc Holliday stood with him."

"And they killed all four?"

"That's right."

"So now I got to worry about Holliday, too?"

"Maybe you should leave town, Dave."

Rudabaugh looked at O'Brien's face in the dim light cast by the storm lamp and said, "You'd like that, wouldn't you, Mike?"

"Hell, Dave—"

"Never mind. I can't leave, anyway. I'm waiting for some boys to meet me here."

"Who?"

"Nobody you know," Rudabaugh said. He ran his thumbnail over his bottom lip and said, "I guess I'll just have to wait until they get here, and then they can help me take care of Earp and Holliday."

"And what about Adams?"

"The Gunsmith? I told you already, Mike. I want that pleasure for myself."

"Sure, Dave—"

"Now get out."

Mike O'Brien backed out of the crib and stopped outside to catch his breath. There was still a chance, he thought. When Rudabaugh faced the Gunsmith, Adams would probably kill him, and then O'Brien wouldn't have to worry anymore.

That is, as long as the Gunsmith won. As long as there was a chance in hell that Rudabaugh could out-draw Adams—who was, after all, a good deal older than Rudabaugh—Mike O'Brien would have to go on living and praying in fear.

After O'Brien left Dave Rudabaugh ate some of the sandwiches the saloon owner had brought him. Munching on them he thought about Wyatt Earp and Doc Holliday. They were supposed to be fast guns, but neither of them had the reputation that the Gunsmith had. Rudabaugh knew that he was taking a chance by choosing the Gunsmith as the one he would face alone, but the rewards were worth the risk. As the man who gunned down Earp or Holliday his reputation would increase only a little from what it now was. However, as the man who gunned down the Gunsmith, the living legend of all gunmen, his reputation would be made.

Rudabaugh was no fool. He knew that other men had tried to outdraw the Gunsmith and had failed, but with this chance at hand, the alternative to failure was large enough to take the risk.

He knew he was fast with a gun and it was about time he found how fast.

He finished the sandwiches without enthusiasm. He was getting real tired of chicken sandwiches and longed for some hot food.

He also wanted another woman, but he was going to have to try and resist that. He hadn't meant to kill that other one, and in fact didn't even remember doing it, but to kill two of them so close together might be dangerous.

Still when that urge welled up inside of him, it was hard to resist . . .

Chapter Sixteen

"Another one?" Doc Gilman asked.

It was the next morning and he had just approached Sheriff Sam Jessup, who was standing outside of a red line crib. Jessup had been called from his office by Talbot, who had explained that another of his girls had been killed. In turn, Jessup had sent for Gilman.

"That's what I'm told," Jessup said.

"Been inside yet?"

Jessup shook his head.

"No, Doc, I got here just a few seconds ahead of you."

"Well, let's go in then."

They entered the crib together and the scene they encountered inside was almost identical to the earlier one. The girl was nude, her face was swollen and bruised and her body was covered with bite marks.

"Jesus," Gilman said. "We got us a crazy, Sam, a plumb loco killer."

"Looks like it."

Gilman bent down to examine the body and Jessup left the crib to talk to Talbot, who was being watched by a deputy.

"Move around and ask some questions, Will," Jessup told the deputy.

"Nobody ever sees nothing, Sam."

"Ask anyway."

The young deputy shrugged and went off to do what he was told.

"What about it, Talbot?" Jessup asked. "Got anything to tell me?"

"Sure, I do. Somebody is trying to put me out of business by killing my girls."

"That's one way of looking at it, I guess," Jessup agreed.

"How would you look at it?"

"Somebody's killing whores, Talbot. The first two just happened to be yours."

"You mean there's gonna be more?"

"Maybe."

"My girls are panicky, Jessup. I ain't gonna be able to keep them on the street. You gotta do something."

"I'm doing the best I can."

"It ain't enough!"

"What would you suggest?"

"Call in the army," Talbot said, waving a hand in the direction of the fort.

"Jesus," Talbot said beneath his breath, that's all he'd need, that asshole Grant down here. "No thanks, I got enough problems."

"Then I'll go and talk to—"

Jessup grabbed Talbot by the front of his shirt and pulled the pimp towards him so that their noses were almost touching.

"This is my town, Talbot. I'm the law here, and I wouldn't take it kindly if you invited anyone else down here to interfere. Do you understand?''

"Sure, Sam, sure," Talbot said, nervously. "I'm just worried, is all."

"You should be," Jessup said, releasing him. "Maybe, when the killer gets his fill of whores, he'll come after the whoremaster. You ever think of that?"

Talbot's eyes popped and he said, "Jesus!"

"Get lost, Talbot," Jessup said. He was disgusted with the man, and with himself for overreacting. "Go and find yourself someplace to hide."

At that point Gilman came out of the crib shaking his head.

"Same as the other one, Sam," he said, rubbing his hand over his unshaven jaw.

"All right, Doc. Thanks."

"I ain't never seen anything like it. This guy must really hate women in general—or maybe just whores."

"What about Talbot?"

Gilman shook his head.

"I ain't no detective, Sam, but if the killer just hated Talbot there'd be no reason for him to do . . . the other things that he's done to the women."

"I guess you're right," Jessup said. "Lord knows, I'm not much of a detective, either."

"I'll have someone come over for the body."

"All right. I'll leave my deputy here to keep the curious away until they get here."

"We never did have that drink after the first one, Sheriff."

"You're right, Doc," Sam said, "and I think this time I'll take you up on it. In a half hour, okay?"

"I'll get a head start on you."

Chapter Seventeen

Clint and Wyatt met in the hotel lobby that morning.

"How was dinner?"

"Fine, just fine," Wyatt said. Apparently, he was going to keep whatever he had discussed with Doc Holliday and Kate Elder to himself. Well, that was his right.

"Did you have breakfast yet?" Clint asked.

"No, and I understand that the Griffin Saloon serves a pretty fair one."

"That's fine with me."

They went over to the saloon where Mike O'Brien was in his customary spot behind the bar.

"I hear you serve breakfast, Mike," Wyatt said.

"Nothing fancy, Mr. Earp. Bacon, eggs, some biscuits, and coffee."

"That sounds good."

"Same for me," Clint said.

"Get yourself a table, then, and I'll bring it over."

They sat at a table and Clint said, "Must be a hell of a breakfast. Look at all these other people!"

The room was empty, except for them.

"Give the man a chance."

O'Brien came out with two plates of runny eggs, burnt bacon, and doughy biscuits.

"Give him a chance, huh?" Clint asked.

Wyatt shrugged and pushed the food around his plate.

Clint poured out the coffee and was pleasantly surprised to find that it was very black, and strong, the way he liked it.

"Well, at least I know where to come for coffee."

As they started eating a small, grizzled looking man in his sixties came in, carrying what looked like a doctor's bag.

"Breakfast, Doc?" Mike O'Brien asked.

"My usual, Michael."

And as Wyatt and Clint watched as the doctor was served his usual breakfast, a shot glass and a bottle of whiskey.

"Remind me not to get hurt in this town," Wyatt said.

"Maybe," Clint said, hopefully, "he's the vet."

"What did you find out last night?"

"Nothing. I walked around and, if anything, this town is wilder at night than in the day time. I was invited into a few dubious-looking poker games, I was propositioned by even more dubious-looking whores, I had a few beers too many, kept my ears open and didn't hear a thing."

"I think we ought to find out today what the names of the men Doc and I killed were. Maybe we can find somebody who knew them, and that way find out who hired them."

"It's as good a course of action as any."

After a few moments Clint looked at Wyatt and asked, "Did you get anything more out of Holliday?"

"Nothing solid, but I'm more convinced than ever that he knows something."

"Sooner or later he'll tell you, then."

"I'm hoping that it'll be sooner.

They were finishing up their breakfast when the sheriff walked into the saloon and took up a position next to the doctor at the bar.

"He doesn't look happy," Clint said.

"Let's find out why not."

They got up and walked to the bar, where the sheriff was joining the doctor in a drink.

"Good morning, Sheriff," Clint said.

"It's anything but that," the sheriff said, unhappily. "Doc, these gentlemen are Wyatt Earp and Clint Adams. This is Doc Gilman."

"I've heard of you gentlemen. Will you join us in a drink?"

"No thanks," Clint said, "we just had one of Mike's breakfasts."

"All the more reason why you should have a drink," the doc said. "It'll kill that breakfast before it kills you."

"Doc . . ." O'Brien complained.

"You don't look happy this morning, Sheriff," Wyatt said. "Any particular reason?"

"We found another dead girl this morning, killed like the last one."

"We've heard stories, Sheriff, but nothing definite . . ." Clint said.

"They were both whores, both beaten to death."

"Anything unusual about the way they were killed?"

Jessup looked at the doc.

"Both of their bodies were covered with bite marks, all of which appear to have been inflicted after death. The killer also had sex with both women, but neither one was alive to enjoy it."

"This fella had sex with them after they were dead?" Wyatt asked.

"That's the way it looks."

"That's sick," Wyatt said.

"That's what I'm dealing with," Jessup said, putting his glass down, "and I'd better get to it. Thanks for the drink, Doc."

"Sheriff, if you're going to your office, I'd like to tag along and get the names of those four men—"

"Come on, then."

"I'll see you later," Wyatt said to Clint, and hurried to catch up with the lawman.

"Join me in a drink, Mr. Adams?" Doc Gilman asked.

"I don't think so, Doc."

"Suit yourself."

"What else can you tell me about these murders, Doc?"

"Not much. Why?"

"I'm curious."

"You'd have to talk to Sam Jessup for the facts—"

"I'm not interested in facts, Doc."

"Supposition?"

Clint nodded.

"Well, I guess there's no harm in that," the little man said. "I've done some reading on the subjects of psychiatry and necromania—"

"Neck-what?"

"Necromania. That's what they call it when some-body would rather have sex with a dead body than a live one."

"I call it crazy."

"That, too, but the killer isn't crazy so much as he is sick," Gilman said, remembering with some em-barrassment his words to Sam Jessup just an hour or so ago. "I tend to forget that, sometimes."

"Could you tell anything by looking at the killer?"

"No," Gilman said. "He'd look as normal as you or me, but I'll tell you one thing. He's beaten two women to death, now, and that's got to have taken a toll on his hands."

"How do you mean?"

"I mean," Gilman said, holding up his own hand, "that he's going to have some damage to his hands. Probably some cuts and bruises on his knuckles."

Neither man saw Mike O'Brien stiffen behind the bar and begin to listen more carefully.

"So if the sheriff finds a man with damage like that to his hands, he might have his killer."

"As long as the man wasn't in a barroom brawl the night before." The doctor pushed away his glass and the half empty bottle and said, "Time for me to get to work, too."

"Have you told the sheriff about the killer's hands?"

"Just a few minutes ago, before you joined us. Mike, thanks for breakfast. Mr. Adams, it was a great pleasure meeting you."

"Same here, Doc."

As the doctor left Clint looked at Mike O'Brien,

who was sweating nervously.

"Something wrong, Mike? You don't look too good."

"Naw—well, I'm just worried. You know, I got a girl working for me—"

"Belinda."

"Yeah. If somebody's killing whores, I'd hate for something to happen to her."

"I don't blame you, Mike. Maybe you should give her some time off."

"Yeah, maybe."

Clint left with the feeling that there was something else on Mike O'Brien's mind, something that was worrying him a lot more than Belinda Darnell's welfare.

After Doc Gilman and Clint Adams left Mike O'Brien leaned on the bar, and tried to catch his breath. He thought back to the night before, when he had brought Dave Rudabaugh the sandwiches. In his mind's eye he saw Rudabaugh reach for the bag with his left hand, and the swollen and cut knuckles of that hand. There were a few different ways that Rudabaugh's hand could have gotten like that, but he had admitted that he'd gone out and got a woman for himself. Had Rudabaugh killed her? And if he had, did that mean that he had killed the second woman, as well? Was he that crazy—or, like the doc said, that sick?

If he was, then Mike O'Brien figured that he had even more reason to be afraid of the man than before.

And he had to work up the courage to do something about it.

•   •   •

It was certainly none of Clint Adams' business, but he found himself fascinated by the murders of the two women. Though not a detective, he had done his share to solve murders in cities like New York and Denver. He wondered how Sam Jessup would feel about an offer of assistance. After all, Wyatt Earp was enlisting Doc Holliday's aid, and Clint certainly felt on more equal terms with Sam Jessup, who was a contemporary of his, than with Holliday, who was younger. For that matter, even though he and Wyatt were friends, Wyatt was more than a dozen years younger, as well. It was only natural that the two younger men should be drawn towards each other. Why shouldn't the two "old timers" work together, as well?

He changed his course and headed for the sheriff's office.

Chapter Eighteen

When he reached Sam Jessup's office Wyatt Earp had already gone. Jessup was seated behind his desk, nursing a cup of coffee with a sour look on his face. Clint wondered whether the sour look came as a result of the coffee, or from the two murders.

"If you're looking for Earp he just left."

"I'm not," Clint said, pulling up a chair, "I was looking for you."

"Want a cup of coffee?"

"Sure."

Jessup got up, got another cup, poured Clint some coffee, handed it to him and then seated himself behind his desk again.

"What's on your mind?"

"These murders."

"What about them?"

"They've got me . . . curious. I wonder what kind of a man it takes to commit two murders like that, and then have his way with the women after they're dead."

"Yeah, that is pretty sick, isn't it?"

"And the odd thing is that he could look as normal as you or me."

"You been talking to the doc?"

"I told you I was curious," Clint said. He sipped the coffee, found it awful and set it down on the edge of the Sheriff's desk. Leaning forward he said, "How about letting me work on this with you?"

"You're working with Earp, aren't you?"

"Doc Holliday's hooked up with him, and I'll be around if he needs me. I'd really like to help you catch this killer."

"Well, I'm no detective, so I can use all the help I can get. I appreciate the offer, Clint."

"You want to fill me in on what you've come up with, so far?"

For the next twenty minutes Jessup told Clint about the two women who had been killed, about the people he had questioned, and about George Talbot, the pimp for whom the two girls worked.

"What about this Talbot? Do you think he could be killing his own girls?"

"I doubt it. For one thing I don't think he's got the nerve. For another, his hands are clean. No bruises, no cuts of any kind."

"Seems to me the first thing you'd have to do is go around town checking people's hands."

"You mean all the men, don't you?"

Clint shrugged and said, "Could be a woman and a man working together. She kills the girl, and the man has his way with the body."

"That'd have to be a pretty sick woman."

"And a pretty strong one. No, I guess your assumption is right. The killer would have to be a man."

"But your idea still applies. I'll have my deputies each take a different section of town and bring in anyone with skinned knuckles."

Clint smiled wryly and said, "In a town like this, where there are ten fights a day, that could amount to a lot of people."

"At least I'll be doing something, and not just sitting here drinking coffee."

"Would you mind if I talked to this George Talbot myself?"

"No, go ahead. Maybe he'll tell you something he won't tell me."

"Where would I find him?"

"Over the red line, in a saloon called the Red Line Palace. He usually hangs around there."

Clint stood up, then turned around and asked, "What about the fort, Sam?"

"What about it?"

"Will you have someone go up there and check out the soldiers' hands?"

Jessup made a face and said, "Then I'd have to deal with that asshole, Colonel Grant."

"We've met him."

"Then you know what I mean." Jessup sighed then and said, "Oh, I guess I'll have to go up there myself and talk to him."

"I'd go with you, but he doesn't like me."

Standing up Jessup said, "He doesn't like anybody, Clint, so don't take it personal."

They walked outside together and Jessup said, "I really do appreciate your offer to help, Clint. You've probably had more experience with this kind of thing than I have. I'm more suited to jailing drunks and breaking up fights."

"I don't think that's exactly the case, Sam, but I'm glad to help."

"I guess you can take the star off the man, but you can't stop being a lawman altogether, huh?"

Clint shrugged and said, "Something like that."

Clint didn't envy Jessup the task of going up to the fort and telling Colonel Grant that one of his men could possibly be a killer. You didn't have to know a man like Grant to predict how he would react.

Clint went back to the hotel to find Wyatt. He wanted to let him know of his offer to help Sheriff Jessup, and reassure him that it would in no way prevent him from helping Wyatt.

Wyatt wasn't at the hotel, so Clint started over to the saloon to see if he was there. On the way he thought of something to check with Wyatt, because Wyatt was the only one who knew anything about Dave Rudabaugh.

Or was he?

For the second time that day he changed direction, this time heading for the telegraph office.

Chapter Nineteen

Eventually, Clint found Wyatt in the saloon, sitting alone over a pot of coffee.

"Swear off the demon drink?"

Wyatt looked up and said, "I just felt like a cup of coffee. Sit and have some."

Since the coffee was the only thing Mike O'Brien seemed to know how to make, Clint agreed. He sat, and O'Brien obligingly brought over another cup.

"Talk to Jessup?"

"Yeah, he gave me the names of the four men Doc and me killed. The leader was called Juice Newton, if you can believe that."

"Never heard of him."

Wyatt told Clint the names of the other three, whom he had likewise never heard of.

"Doc said he'd check around and see if they had any friends in town."

"Fine."

"What have you been doing?"

"I've been talking to Jessup, too, Wyatt. I'm curious about these murders and I'd like to try and help him solve them. Of course, that doesn't mean I won't be around if you need me," he added quickly.

"That's OK with me, Clint," Wyatt said. "You

aren't bound to me by any contract other than friendship. I appreciate that you came all this way with me. If you want to help Jessup, that's fine with me. I'd like to see that mad dog caught, too."

"Speaking of mad dogs," Clint said, "what can you tell me about Dave Rudabaugh?"

"Not much. I hadn't heard of him before he held up that train. Apparently somebody on board recognized him, and that's how the railroad got his name to give to me."

"You don't know what kind of man he is?"

"He's a lawbreaker," Earp said, "that was all I needed to know."

Clint frowned at the reply, but said nothing.

"What I'm trying to get at is, is he the kind of man who could have committed these murders?"

"The two whores? What makes you think that?"

"Because they happened after we—and Rudabaugh, supposedly—got here."

Wyatt rubbed his jaw and said, "I can't answer that, Clint. Like I said, I don't know anything about him."

"Well, I've sent a telegram to someone who might." When Wyatt frowned Clint said, "Rick Hartman, in Labyrinth. If anyone has the contacts to find out about Rudabaugh, he does."

Wyatt nodded and looked as if he had something on his mind.

"You know, I get paid more if I bring him back."

"And?"

"And if he turns out to be the killer, they're gonna want him here."

"Why should that matter? You said yourself you weren't fanatical about bringing him back."

"Sure, if I can't find him I'm not going to spend

the rest of my life looking, but if I do find him that's a different story. If I find him, I want him.''

"And if he is the killer, and Jessup finds him?"

Wyatt didn't like the question and said simply, ''In that case, we'd have to see.''

Clint didn't like the sound of that.

"Are you mad?"

The question came from Colonel Charles L. Grant, directed at Sheriff Sam Jessup.

"I'm just telling you that's one of the possibilities, Colonel.''

"You're telling me that one of my men is a killer of women, of common whores?''

"I'm telling you that it could be one of your men. It could also be someone from the Flat—''

"Well, if you ask me your best bet is to look among that rabble, and not among honorable members of the United States Army. I don't intend to have my men submit to an inspection of their hands, for God's sake.''

"All I'm asking is some cooperation, Colonel,'' Jessup said, wearily. "I don't want to have to go over your head to get it.''

Grant stuck his jaw out stubbornly and said, "You do that, civilian, you go over my head!''

Jessup considered continuing the argument and then just decided that the whole thing had been a mistake.

"Very well, Colonel, if that's the way you want it.''

The Sheriff turned and left the Colonel's office.

Chapter Twenty

Later that evening, Clint found his way to the **Red Line Palace** easily. He'd waited the evening to go there, figuring his best chance of finding the pimp Talbot was during the man's working hours, which were after dark.

Several girls approached Clint on the street and he wondered idly how many of them worked for Talbot.

The Red Line Palace wasn't much of a palace, but that didn't stop the mob of people who were there from having a good time. Clint had to force his way to the bar, and as he pushed forward clearing a path the crowd closed in behind him again, effectively cutting him off from the entrance.

When he reached the bar he ordered a beer and waited for the bartender to bring it before he asked for Talbot. He felt there was no harm in asking for the man straight out. He'd probably just look like a man seeking a good time.

"Talbot?" the bartender shouted to be heard above the din caused by loud piano music and even louder voices. Clint nodded and the man said, "In the back!"

"Which way's the back?"

The bartender grinned and pointed. Clint signalled his thanks, then decided to finish the beer before trying to get through the crowd.

Clint had the impression that a space had been cleared in the center of the place—or *palace*—for some reason, and asked the man next to him about it.

"Estralita is dancing," the man said.

"Who's Estralita?"

The man looked at him as if he were crazy and then they were suddenly separated by a tide of humanity. They had all apparently done this before, for in no time all the occupants of the place were spread out into a circle and, standing only three deep, everyone had an even chance of seeing Estralita's dance.

Clint was fortunate enough to be standing behind two short men—or perhaps that, too, was a result of practice—and he was able to see what all the commotion was about.

Estralita stood in the center of the room, hands firmly planted on wide hips, her large round breasts barely contained by a low cut peasant blouse. Standing still she was beautiful, with long, black hair and dark skin, but when she started to move he realized what the excitement was really about.

When the music started and she began to dance, she went from beautiful to breathtaking. The energy she gave off was almost electric, like lightning. As she whirled and danced her breasts bounced almost free of her blouse, and her skirt swirled to reveal taut, muscular thighs and legs.

Clint watched her along with everyone else, his real reason for being there forgotten for those few minutes. She circled the room, giving every man in the place a chance for a close look at her, and then at the end a path opened for her almost magically and she went through a curtained doorway in the rear.

"That," the bartender said, leaning over the bar, "was Estralita."

"It certainly was," Clint said. He turned to face the man and asked, "Now can you tell me which one is Talbot?"

Before the crowd could close back in towards the center of the floor the bartender pointed to a tall man with slicked down hair wearing a dark suit, seated alone at a table against the back wall.

"That's George Talbot."

"Thanks."

The bartender touched Clint's arm before he could move away and said, "And those are Mr. Talbot's . . . friends." The bartender's tone made it clear that "friends" in this case meant bodyguards. Talbot was apparently taking the murders of his girls to heart.

"Sitting at the table behind him, or in front of him?"

"Both."

"He must be a pretty nervous man to need so many. . . friends."

"He's got call to be."

"Yes, I guess he has. Thanks, again."

Clint started to move across the floor just as the waves of humanity began to sweep back in. He got jolted and jostled a few times but for the most part made the trip unharmed.

As he approached George Talbot's table he noticed that the two men seated behind him and the two ahead of him suddenly came to attention. They were all hard cases of the type Clint had seen many times in many towns, looking for jobs they could do with their fists or their guns, without much strain on their brains.

"Excuse me, are you Mr. Talbot?"

Talbot, a man in his late thirties by all appearances, looked up with a bored expression on his face.

"I'm Talbot. You looking for some company, friend?"

"Seems to me, Mr. Talbot, that's a pretty dangerous question for you to be asking these days."

Talbot looked at his bodyguards swiftly, saw that they were in place, and then said, "Is that a threat?"

"No, it's not a threat. In fact, I wasn't even talking about danger to yourself. I was speaking more of danger to your girls."

"Are you the low life that's been killing my girls?" Talbot asked, a trace of nervousness creeping into his voice.

Clint saw that unless he soothed Talbot's fears he was about a minute away from tangling with the man's four . . . friends.

"I think you misunderstand me, Mr. Talbot. My name is Clint Adams, and I'm helping the sheriff in the investigation of the murder of the two girls."

"Are you his deputy?"

"No, I'm not."

Talbot shrugged and said, "Then I don't have to talk to you, do I?"

"No, you don't, but if you don't talk to me here you'll have to talk to me at the sheriff's office—with the sheriff present."

Clint had guessed that Talbot feared Sam Jessup. He could see it in the man's face.

"Why are you interested in finding out who killed my girls?"

"I'm curious about what kind of man could do something like that."

"Curious, huh?" Talbot asked, glancing at his

bodyguards. "I'm curious, too. I'm curious to see if he'll bleed like everyone else when he's full of bullet holes."

"Is that what your friends are here for? To see that he gets filled with bullet holes?"

"If he comes anywhere near me."

"Why would he do that—listen, do you mind if I sit down?"

Talbot thought a moment, then nodded and said, "Go on, sit down."

Clint sat and turned his chair so that his back was to the wall. He could see the rest of the room, and he could keep an eye on all four bodyguards. He asked the question again.

"Why would he come after you?"

"He's killing my girls, isn't he? That means he's got something against me, doesn't it?"

"Not necessarily. Maybe he had something against those particular girls. Or maybe he's got something against women in general."

"You think so? Jesus, it was Jessup who said he'd probably come after me, sooner or later."

"Well, that's a theory of the sheriff's. I happen to think you're in the clear."

"Oh yeah?" Talbot asked, grasping at the straw. "What makes you say that?"

Talbot's hands were on the table in plain sight and Clint looked down at them. They were clean, well cared for hands. The hands of a vain man, with not a mark on them. Clint wondered how he'd be able to get a look at the hands of the other four men before he left.

"I think that the killer is killing whores, and that it's just a coincidence that the two he's killed so far were your girls."

"So far? You mean you think he'll kill more?"

"Don't you? He's a madman, isn't he? I don't think he'll stop until somebody stops him."

"Like you?"

"Or maybe you?"

"Me?"

"Don't you want him stopped?"

"Sure, but—"

"Isn't he hurting your business?"

"Well, yeah, but—"

"Don't you want to prove to the sheriff that you're not the killer?"

"Me? Jessup think I killed my own girls?"

Clint shrugged and said, "It's just another theory of his."

"Why would I kill my own girls?"

"Because you'd be the least logical person to do it."

"Why would I hire bodyguards and fear for my own life if I killed them?"

"To cover up. To make it look like you're afraid of the killer when you *are* the killer."

"That's crazy!"

"Ah, but we're talking about a madman, aren't we?"

"Jesus," Talbot said, rubbing one hand over his face, "now I not only have to worry about the killer, I've got to worry about a sheriff who thinks I *am* the killer."

"Like I said, it's just a th—"

"Jessup never liked me, that's what it is. He wants to blame me for this."

"Maybe I can help you."

"Why would you help me?"

"I want to see the killer caught, Talbot, that's why."

"I don't trust you," Talbot said after a few moments.

"That's fine," Clint said, standing up. "Don't trust anyone. Or better yet, trust these gunhawks you've hired. They've got enough brain between them to thread a needle."

"Now wait a minute—" one of the men said, standing up. He apparently took offense at what Clint had said.

"Sit down," Talbot said.

"He can't—"

"Sit down!" Talbot snapped, giving the man a hard look. He looked back at Clint and said, "Give me some time to think it over."

"How much time?"

"Meet me here tomorrow night."

"Fine," Clint said, "you better just hope there's not a murder tonight."

He left the saloon, feeling that he had learned a lot about George Talbot. When the man was in his own element—dealing with his whores, or his employees —he was hard and tough, but when it came to dealing with Jessup, or an unseen killer, the man became a coward.

This meant that deep inside of him the man was a natural coward, and Clint just didn't think that such a man could have committed the gruesome murders of those two women.

He might, however, help catch him.

Chapter Twenty-One

After Clint Adams left George Talbot sent one of his friends out to find out where the Gunsmith was staying, and another into the back to get Estralita. When she arrived he had a bottle of whiskey and two glasses waiting on the table.

"Sit down, Lita."

"What is it, Talbot?" she asked, her English slightly accented. "I have to dance again later."

"You dance because I say you dance for a living instead of fucking for one. I could change my mind, you know—especially if you forget your place."

Estralita Velez hated George Talbot, but she feared him even more. She was twenty-four, and for four years she had been just one of his whores. That is, until he found out that she could dance.

She never wanted to be "just one of his whores" again.

"I'm sorry, George," she said, lowering her head. Once, just to make sure she still knew her place, he made her take on all of his bodyguards one after the other, and she never wanted to repeat that degrading experience again.

"That's better, Lita, but I still think you need a little lesson."

"No, George," she said, lifting her head and looking right at him. "Please. Not again—"

"Oh, stop worrying, Estralita," he said, patting her hand. "I only want you to visit a man for me." He held up a finger for her to see and said, "Just one man."

"Who?"

"His name is Clint Adams and he's a very famous man, a legend."

"What kind of a legend?" she asked, curious in spite of herself.

"A gunfighter, a killer. They call him the Gunsmith. Have you ever heard of him?"

"Of course," she said. "Everyone has heard of the Gunsmith."

"Well, I want you to go to the hotel and stay with him tonight. Find out why he's here, what he's looking for."

"I can't just go to him and say I want to stay with him—"

"Of course you can. He was here watching you dance, he won't turn you away." Instead of patting one of her hands this time he took it in his and held it. It took will power, but she restrained herself from pulling it away. "How could any man turn you away?"

"What am I to tell him?"

"Tell him you saw him watching you and you wanted him. No man could disbelieve that. His ego will not let him."

George Talbot was in his element, now. He knew

what men thought and what they felt and he taught his girls how to play on that.

And the Gunsmith was, after all, just a man.

"Go and get yourself ready. When you come back I will tell you where he is staying."

"Yes, George."

Estralita went to her room in the back, her dressing room, she called it, like in the theater, and sat in a straight-backed chair, staring into the mirror. She examined herself critically. Her nostrils flared too much, although she knew men liked that. They thought it meant she was passionate. Her mouth was too wide, she thought, but again, she had never had any complaints. Her best features, she thought, were her hair and her legs. Her hair was rich and full and as black as night, and her legs were long and muscled. She knew, too, that she had good breasts, but they were too large for a dancer and she sometimes wished they were smaller.

She stood up and undressed so she could examine herself naked. She was beautiful, and she knew it, but she was also very frightened. She would not know how to care for herself on her own, so she stayed with George Talbot and did what he told her. At least she did not have to whore, anymore—not very often, anyway. When Talbot discovered how men loved to watch her dance, how the fact that she seemed unattainable to them made them love to watch even more, he took her off the streets and out of the cribs.

Lita had one real friend in town and that was Belinda Darnell. She wished she could be like

Belinda. She worked for Mike O'Brien, but she was really independent and hardly ever had to sleep with anyone for money.

Lita examined her full breasts and her smooth buttocks for sags and, finding none, dressed to go and meet this legend, the Gunsmith.

She had never slept with a legend before. Would he be different, she wondered, or would he be just like any other man without his guns on?

She convinced herself that this was not whoring, that she was doing this to satisfy her own curiosity. That done, she began to feel a tingle of excitement.

Chapter Twenty-Two

When the knock came at the door Clint Adams had just removed his boots. His gunbelt was on the bedpost and he took out the .45 and held it in his hand as he approached the door.

"Who is it?"

"Estralita," a woman's voice said. He frowned for a moment, and then she said, "The dancer, Señor."

The dancer from the saloon? What was she doing here?

He opened the door, saw her standing there and then looked to either side of her.

"I am quite alone," she said. "May I come in?"

"Of course, come in," he said, standing to one side to allow her to enter. He gave the hall a quick look before closing the door.

"You will not need the gun," she assured him. "I will not hurt you."

Instead of replying to the barb he simply returned the gun to the holster on the bedpost and then turned to face her.

"I saw you dance tonight," he said. "You were magnificent."

"I am glad you felt that way, Señor Adams," she

said. "I saw you tonight, as well, and had similar thoughts."

"Really?" Clint asked, not believing her for a moment.

"Yes, I ask around to find out who you were, and they told me that you are a legend. Is this true?"

"It is a truth based on falsehood."

"Please—" she said, frowning.

"I'll explain it to you sometime. Why don't you tell me who sent you here, Estralita? Was it George Talbot?"

"Señor, Talbot?" she asked, her frown deepening. "Why would he send me?"

"To find out what I want, why I'm here. Maybe to see if I'm not after him for something."

"I do not understand—"

"Sure, you do. I'd be willing to bet that Talbot owns the saloon you dance at, and I'd be just as willing to bet that he owns you."

"No man owns me!"

Her reaction was too swift, too angry.

"Do you tell yourself that, Estralita? Really?"

She glared at him boldly, and then her boldness melted away. She was wearing a knitted shawl over a low cut dress and he could see the swell of her breasts beneath it.

"If he sent you here to sleep with me that's fine, Estralita. I'd like that very much. But if you're looking for information, I can give you that and you can leave."

"Give me—you mean, you would tell me what he wants to know and let me leave? You wouldn't make me lie down with you, first?"

"Not first and not after. I've never forced a woman to have sex with me, and I've never paid a woman. I haven't ever had to do either."

This was a different man, she thought.

"And if I chose to stay?"

"We would enjoy each other very much, Estra-lita."

"Even though you know I work for Talbot?"

"Even so."

"I do not understand you."

"I'm not so hard to understand. I have an opportunity to sleep with a beautiful and exciting woman. I don't want to waste it or ruin the experience with lies."

"You are a strange man."

"What does Talbot want to know, Estralita?"

"Please, call me Lita. He wants to know why you are in town."

"I'm helping a friend look for a man, a criminal who robbed a train."

"You are not here to harm him?"

"Not at all. I only met him because I would like to help the sheriff find the murderer of the two girls. Did you know them, Lita?"

"I knew them."

"Did either one of them mention being frightened of anyone? Of being followed at all?"

"If they had those fears they would have told George Talbot. He would have had his men take care of it. They did not mention any such fears to me."

"I see. Is there anything else you would like to know for Talbot?"

She started to speak, then stopped and said, "No, nothing more. I am not longer here for Talbot. I am here for myself."

"Good," he said.

He stepped forward and lifted the shawl from her

shoulders, dropping it to the floor. Her breasts were dark and there was a musky natural fragrance coming from her. It excited him. He remembered how she had looked dancing and that excited him even more.

He leaned over and kissed her wide mouth. Her tongue entered his mouth tentatively at first, and then more forcefully. The kiss did not involve their hands or any other part of their bodies at all, just their mouths and tongues. When he pulled away he saw that her eyes were shiny and her nostrils were flared.

"You are very, very beautiful," he said.

"My mouth is too wide," she said, kissing him, "and my nostrils are funny—"

"They are wonderful," he said, kissing her nose.

He moved his hands to her waist now and pulled her closer. When they kissed this time it was with their entire bodies. His hands cupped her buttocks while her arms went around his waist. Her breasts were crushed against his chest and their crotches were pressed tightly together. Her musky scent seemed to grow stronger. He moved his hands up to entangle them in her hair and kissed her neck. Her breath came quickly as she dug her nails into his back through his shirt.

"It's time to undress," he said.

"Yes," she said, unbuttoning his shirt, "it is time . . ."

When they were undressed they took a moment to look at each other. He marvelled at the tautness of her body. Her breasts were large, yet firm and unsagging. Her waist was small, her belly was convex, her navel deep, her pubic hair a dark, tangled jungle. Her legs, the legs he had glimpsed during her dance, he now examined at his leisure. They were long and smooth, well muscled and graceful.

Lita examined Clint Adams and found him very pleasing. He was tall and slim, yet there was muscle there, well-toned muscle. His stomach was perhaps not as flat as it had once been, but he was a fine figure of a man. His face was not handsome, especially with the curious Y-shaped scar on his left cheek, but it was a kind and pleasing face.

She looked at his tumid cock then and, going to her knees, reached for it.

He watched her as first she used her hair on him. She picked it up in both her hands and swirled it around him, allowing her tongue to make only fleeting contact. When she had him aroused to bursting she reached behind him to cup his buttocks and pull him to her, and opened her mouth wide to accommodate him. Her head bobbed as her mouth rode him wetly and she squeezed his buttocks as he took her head in his hands and suddenly he exploded, filling her mouth. She groaned and accepted all he had to give her, then smiled at him and kissed his belly again and again with her hot mouth.

She used her hands to tickle him and caress him, then used her mouth to suckle him and incredibly she aroused him once again.

He turned her towards the bed and pushed her down gently onto it. She put her hands over her head so that her breasts lifted and he kissed them lovingly, licking them and sucking the nipples, gently at first, then harder while his fingers probed through her pubic patch. She felt his fingers deftly parting her and then entering her and she lifted her hips to meet him. He was still sucking her breasts as his fingers —first one, then a second—delved deeply into her warmth. She moaned and bucked as he continued his dual ministrations, drawing her body as taut as a

guitar string, and then he was kissing her belly, prob-
ing her navel with his tongue, digging his nose into
her black jungle. His fingers withdrew and she felt
his tongue replace it, licking her, moving over her,
parting her, entering her . . .

Her musky odor was stronger still as he ran his
tongue over her. It seemed to fill his nostrils and play
havoc with his senses. She gasped and arched her
back when his tongue slid out and over her clit, and
he felt it rigid and wanting. He pursed his lips and
sucked it gently, then circled it with his tongue. Her
hips moved in unison with the movement of his
tongue, and he slid his hands beneath her so he could
cradle her buttocks. He lifted her so that he could get
better access and ran his tongue over her completely
again, getting as much of her tartness as he could on
the outside, dipping inside her for more, and then
centering once again on her taut clit, sucking, licking,
flicking, until suddenly she went rigid. He felt a
tremor in her belly and then she was writhing beneath
him and he had to fight to keep his mouth in contact
with her. He continued to lick her and she moaned
and cried out in Spanish. She reached for him frantically and as he climbed atop her she gathered him to
her, encircling him with her arms and legs as he
entered her deeply . . .

His only concern seemed to be for her pleasure,
and she had never encountered that in a man before.

He was indeed different, she thought happily as he
drove himself into her and kissed her, very different . . .

They made love twice more before morning and

then, as the light filtered into the room through the window, Clint watched as Lita stretched, naked on the bed, her muscles tensing and relaxing, and felt himself growing hard again . . .

After they made love for a fourth time and were lying side by side she said, "I feel wonderful. I do not feel like going back to George Talbot."

"I wish I could say you didn't have to."

She looked at him and asked, "Do you want me to go back and get some information for you?"

"I wouldn't ask you to do that for me, Lita. What I need from Talbot I can get myself."

"He is afraid of you, you know."

"He's afraid of anyone he can't control. He'd be afraid of you if you left him."

"If I left him," she said ashamed, "I would be afraid."

"How long have you been with him?"

"Since my mother died. I was fourteen. She was forty-five and whoring for him and when she was gone he taught me."

"The bastard!"

"When he saw how men reacted when I danced, he took me away from that and told me I would only have to dance."

"He lied."

She shrugged and said, "A little."

"He sent you to me."

"Once in a while he says he likes to remind me of my place."

"Leave him, Lita."

"I haven't the courage," she said, sadly. "I have never been on my own."

He felt a little like he had felt with Belinda Darnell, like Lita might have been asking him to take her with him when he left, only he didn't think it was intentional on her part. Of Belinda he could believe that she would ask him, but not Lita.

It was a shame, though, that Lita would never become the wonderful person she could have been if she left George Talbot—unless she worked up the courage to leave.

He took her in his arms and held her, holding back the urge to say, "Leave him, Lita, and come with me." He did not want the responsibility of someone else's life, right now, especially someone as vulnerable and open to hurt as Lita Velez obviously was. If he asked her to leave with him she would not understand that it was not out of love, and therein lay the potential for even more hurt.

"When you go back to Talbot," he said, "just tell him the truth about why I'm here."

"Yes."

She didn't even question whether or not he was telling *her* the truth. She accepted that he was.

If she left Talbot she'd never have to whore for a living—not the way she danced. In that respect she was ahead of Belinda Darnell, but she needed some of the other woman's toughness.

There had to be some way of getting her to leave Talbot and go out on her own.

Chapter Twenty-Three

After Lita left, Clint gathered up some clean clothes and went downstairs for a bath. As he was leaving the hotel he was preoccupied with the subject of Lita Velez and almost walked past Wyatt Earp.

"Hey!"

Brought out of his reverie by the greeting, Clint looked at Wyatt and said, "Oh, good morning."

"Where were you just now?"

"What?"

"You looked like you were a thousand miles away."

"Oh, I was just thinking."

"And I know what about."

"Oh, what?"

"I saw that woman leave your room this morning. Where did you find her?"

"She's a dancer at the Red Line Palace."

"Well, she's worth thinking about, I'll tell you that."

"How are you getting along with Doc?"

"Pretty good, I guess, but I can't seem to break through, get him to trust me enough to tell me what he knows."

"Why not try Kate Elder?"

Wyatt thought about it for a moment, then said, "That's an idea."

"Want some breakfast?"

"Not at the saloon. I'm not ready to try one of Mike O'Brien's specialties again."

"There's got to be someplace in town besides this hotel and the saloon to get breakfast. Let's take a look."

They'd each been around town often enough, but they hadn't been looking for someplace to eat. A few blocks away they found a cafe that seemed to be doing a brisk business. They entered, got a table and ordered.

"I'm tempted to go over to the sheriff's office and find out if there was another murder last night," Clint said.

"How are you coming with that?"

"I talked to the man who the two girls worked for. He's nervous and I think he'll talk to me tonight."

"What makes you say that?"

"I told him I wanted to help him, and he checked me out last night. He'll talk to me."

"Did you get an answer to your telegram about Rudabaugh, yet?"

"Not yesterday. I'll check the telegraph office after breakfast, and then go and see the sheriff."

"If there had been another murder I think we would have heard it on the street."

"I think you're right," Clint said as breakfast came. It *looked* better than what Mike O'Brien had served them, but they wouldn't be able to tell without tasting.

"Well," Clint said, taking a deep breath to

prepare himself, "let's give this one a shot and see what happens."

The breakfast was fine, but when it came to the coffee Clint was disappointed.

"O'Brien's was better than this."

"Maybe you should eat breakfast here and then go over there for coffee."

"I guess so, unless we can find one place that has both."

They drank their coffee anyway and then paid their bill. As they approached the door to leave Wyatt put his hand on Clint's arm.

"I suppose you know that we were followed from the hotel."

Clint nodded. He had seen the man as soon as he and Wyatt had started from the hotel.

"Know him?" Wyatt asked.

"He works for Talbot. He was with him at the Red Line Palace last night."

"Hired gun?"

"Bodyguard. I think he usually has some men on the payroll for strongarm stuff, but now he's nervous and he's hired some extra help."

"You want to brace him?"

Clint shook his head.

"He won't bother you. When we split up he'll stay with me, and I'm not going anywhere I don't want Talbot to know about."

They stepped outside and, looking directly at the man who was making no attempt to disguise his purpose, he said, "If he stays on me all day, he's going to have a pretty boring day."

Chapter Twenty-Four

George Talbot was in his room above the Red Line Saloon when there was a knock on his door. The two bodyguards in the room with him immediately moved for the door with their guns out. One pressed himself against the wall and the other one swung it open.

"Talbot?" Lita Velez said.

"It's all right, boys," George Talbot said, walking to the door. "It's just my number one girl." He took her hand and said, 'Come on in, Lita. Would you like some coffee?"

"Yes, please," she said, hesitantly. She was always leery of Talbot when he was being a gentleman. It usually preceded a slap in the face.

The bodyguards closed the door and went back to their own coffee which they had been having at a table set up in a corner. Talbot's table was in the center of the room, and would be removed when he finished his breakfast.

"Sit down, Lita."

She sat, still watching him, nervously.

He poured her a cup of coffee and placed it in front of her.

"There. Now that we've seen to the amenities,

what have you to tell me about our mutual friend, Mr. Adams?''

"He's here to help a friend of his find a man who held up a train.''

"What friend?''

"Wyatt Earp.''

Talbot's eyebrows went up and he said, "Another fabled gentleman, though certainly not in the class of the Gunsmith." He looked at one of the bodyguards and inclined his head. The man left to find out about Wyatt Earp. "Did you believe him?''

"Yes.''

"Did this information come to you by virtue of, uh, pillow talk?''

She lowered her head and said, "Yes.''

"What's this, shyness?''

"No.''

"It's not out of character, Lita. I know that you're basically shy—except when you're dancing, that is.''

"Yes.''

"You are also agreeable this morning. That, I'm afraid, is out of character.''

He stood up, rounded the table and took her face in his hand, pinching her cheeks together.

"Did you like Mr. Adams?''

"Yes!" she said, defiantly.

"And I suppose he told you he would take you with him when he left?''

"No,'' she said, and her tone was such that he believed her.

"Oh ho,'' he said, releasing her face, "is that why you are so depressed this morning. Mr. Adams succumbed to your charms, but only momentarily.''

She didn't reply.

"What are his intentions towards me?"

"He has none. He wants only to help Sheriff Jessup find the murderer of the two girls."

"And you believed him?"

"Yes."

He took her chin in his hand and tilted her face up.

"You had better be right, Lita."

Again, she didn't reply.

"All right, get out. Get some rest, I want you to dance well tonight."

"I dance well every night," she said, and was rewarded with a resounding slap that made the bodyguard in the corner jump.

"Don't be insolent! Now get out."

She stood up, turned and walked out. He watched her with mixed feelings, not the least of which was lust.

He sat down to finish his breakfast and was pouring another cup of coffee when the other bodyguard returned.

"What?" Talbot said.

"Wyatt Earp is in town looking for a man named Dave Rudabaugh. Adams rode in with him and is supposed to be helping him, but Earp has been seen in with Doc Holliday, lately."

"All right," Talbot said, putting his cup down. "It looks like Mr. Adams is on the level about this, although God knows why. I don't see what he plans to get out of it, but if he can find this maniac killer, then let him."

The bodyguards remained silent because they knew Talbot wasn't talking to them. When he spoke to them he looked at them, and he did that now.

"When he shows up tonight bring him up here."

"You gonna help him?"

"In every way I can," Talbot said, "and in doing so I'll be helping myself. Finding this killer will get him *and* Jessup off my back."

"The sheriff doesn't look so tough," one of the bodyguards said. Talbot didn't see which one had spoken, but it didn't matter. They were virtually interchangeable. In fact, they were just what Clint Adams had said they were.

"He'd kill either one of you—or both—without blinking an eye."

And me, too, Talbot thought, given half the chance.

"I'd like to try him," one of them said, and the other nodded.

Talbot started to answer then stopped, struck by the germ of an idea.

What if these two idiots did try Jessup? What did Talbot have to lose? Two bodyguards who could be replaced very easily.

On the other hand, what did he have to gain if they succeeded in killing the lawman? He would get Jessup off his back for good, which was something he'd wanted for a long time. He hated Jessup more than any man alive because he was afraid of him— and Jessup knew it!

Then again, if Jessup was killed in some other way—say, from ambush some night while making his rounds—who would get the blame? The whore killer, that's who. It made sense.

Sitting back and lighting a cigar Talbot started to think that even though he'd lost two girls, this situation could be turned to his advantage. With the Gunsmith on the trail of the killer, Talbot could concentrate on putting Sam Jessup out of the way and shifting the blame on the mad dog killer everyone knew was in town.

The only thing he had to make sure of was that he got Jessup before the Gunsmith got the killer.

Estralita Velez had a room on the same floor. After she left she hurried down the hall, her face stinging, opened her door and slammed it behind her. She looked around the room, hating it more now than ever.

She sat in front of her mirror and examined the outline of George Talbot's hand in angry red on her cheek. She was concerned about whether or not she would bruise.

Trying to rub the redness away, she swore it would be the last time he ever struck her.

Chapter Twenty-Five

After breakfast Clint stopped off at the telegraph office to see if there was a reply from Rick Hartman yet. Talbot's bodyguard followed along.

"Came in early this morning when I opened up, Mr. Adams," the operator said.

Clint thanked him and took the telegram with him to his hotel. There was a chair out front so he sat down and opened the telegram and read Rick's reply.

DAVE RUDABAUGH DANGEROUS MAN. STRING OF UNSOLVED MURDERS OF WOMEN BEHIND HIM. NO PROOF. BY THE WAY, GOOD WITH A GUN, HAS FRIENDS IN TEXAS. LUCK.

HARTMAN

Well, it wasn't proof, but it was something to think about. He folded up the message, tucked it into his shirt pocket and went over to see if Jessup was in his office.

Sam Jessup woke that morning with a feeling of foreboding. Pulling on his boots he wondered if the women of the Flat had gotten through the night alive.

Jessup slept in one of the cells behind his office, because the people of the Flat had not seen fit to furnish him with a place to live, and his salary certainly didn't give him many options.

How does a promising young lawman come to this, he wondered, and then decided that he had enough depressing thoughts that morning without adding to them.

Clint entered the sheriff's office just as Jessup was pouring a cup of coffee from the office pot.

"Care for a cup?" he asked Clint.

"Sure," Clint said, looking out the window. "I'm game."

"What are you looking at?"

"I've got somebody following me," Clint said, "and I don't want to lose them."

Jessup poured one and then brought both to the desk. "I guess I'm not meant to understand that. Did you talk to Talbot?"

"I did. He's checking me out, and he's the one having me followed, but I think he's going to cooperate with me."

"In what way?"

"Well, for one thing he's got to do something to protect his girls, like having them work in twos."

"That sounds interesting," Jessup admitted, sipping his coffee.

"Most of all I just want him to trust me."

"Fat chance of that since you're working with me. Talbot and I aren't exactly the best of friends."

"How long has he been working the Flat?"

"Since before I came here. Had it pretty easy too until then."

"Is he a pet project of yours?"

"I don't like anyone who degrades women. That goes for Talbot, and for this crazy killer—if they're not one and the same."

"Are you serious about that?"

"I don't know," Jessup said, wearily rubbing a hand over his face. "I haven't had to deal with anything like this before. Maybe I'm grasping at straws."

"Well, I've got something a little more substantial than straws for you," Clint said, taking the telegram from Rick Hartman out of his pocket. "Try that."

"What is it?" Jessup asked, reaching across the desk for it.

"Read it."

Clint waited, sipping the sheriff's dangerous brew gingerly while the lawman read the passage.

"This changes things," Jessup said, putting the telegram down. "At least we know who we're looking for now."

"Now, there's never been any proof against him before, Sam, and there's no proof now that he's the one who killed those girls."

"Well, there's no harm in looking for him. Has your friend Earp got any leads?"

"One. He thinks that Holliday might know something important."

"Well then, let's go and talk to Holliday," Jessup said, rising.

"I think we should let Wyatt handle Holliday in his own way, Sam. Why don't we concentrate on Talbot."

"You just said—"

"I still think he can help us catch the killer. Let me

think about it some today and talk to him tonight. If he took all of his girls off the street and out of the cribs—"

"If? That'd mean a night with no money for Talbot. He'd never stand for that. He'd rather lose a girl a night and turn a profit."

"I think he'll do what I ask him to do."

"Why?"

"Because if he's not the killer he's going to figure I'm his best chance to get rid of him for him. He wants business to go back to being as usual—don't you?"

"Sure. I'd rather have to deal with Talbot than with some mad killer."

"Okay then, let Wyatt work on Holliday, and let me work on Talbot."

"And what do I work on while you're doing all this?"

"Well, for one thing you could find out if there was another murder last night."

"I'd say no, or I would have heard about it by now, but if you want we can check."

Clint put his coffee down, virtually untouched, and said, "Let's go." Rising, Jessup said, "If you're going to accept my coffee the least you could do is drink it."

"Accepting it isn't dangerous . . ."

They went over the Red Line and walked among the cribs and it was obvious that the night had passed uneventfully—as far as murder was concerned, anyway. Talbot's bodyguard seemed nervous about following Clint *and* the sheriff, but he did it, anyway.

"Maybe the guy left town," Jessup said, his tone hopeful.

"I doubt that."

"Why?"

"He's had easy pickings here so far," Clint said, waving a hand to indicate the cribs. "Why stop now? Why leave? He's got to think that things are going his way."

"Aren't they?"

"Sure," Clint said, "now, but not for long."

"Right, not for long . . ."

"Why don't we go and talk to the doctor," Clint suggested. "Maybe he'll be able to tell us something that will help us."

"Sure." Jessup was less then enthusiastic.

"Besides," Clint added, "his coffee has got to be better than yours."

"Want to bet?"

Chapter Twenty-Six

Although Doc Holliday still had not confided in Wyatt Earp, the two men had become fast friends in just a few days.

For Earp's part, he felt that Holliday could be as good a friend to him as Bat Masterson. They were of comparable age and lifestyle, and to date Masterson had been the only man—besides his own brothers and Clint Adams—Wyatt could stand to be around.

Holliday, on the other hand, had for some reason developed a sort of hero worship for the slightly older Wyatt Earp. It was something that neither he nor Kate Elder understood.

Not only did Kate not understand, however, but she also disapproved.

"You going to see Wyatt Earp again?" she asked that morning.

"I suppose."

"Are you going to tell him about Mike O'Brien?"

Holliday hesitated, then said, "Probably."

"I don't think you should."

"Why not?"

Holliday had been sitting at the kitchen table in his shirtsleeves, finishing his coffee, and now he stood up and strapped on his gun.

"Mike's been good to you."

"I'm not doing anything to hurt Mike. In fact, if he knows where Rudabaugh is, I'm doing him a favor, and if he doesn't, I'm not doing him any harm."

"So you just want to do Wyatt Earp a favor, is that it?"

"Yes, I suppose that's it."

"I don't know what it is about that man that fascinates you so. I suppose when he leaves you're going to want to ride with him."

"I didn't say that."

"And where would that leave me?"

Holliday slipped into his jacket and looked at the woman who loved him.

"I guess that would leave you here, Kate, unless you wanted to come, too."

"You have a good life here, Doc," she argued. "*We* have a good life here."

"I didn't say I was leaving."

"You don't have to say it, I can see it in your eyes. You want to ride with him and get yourself killed."

"I'm dying anyway, Kate, and I think that by staying here I'm dying a little faster. I want to live some, Kate, before I die."

"The kind of life that Wyatt Earp lives?"

"Why not? What's wrong with that?"

"That kind of life usually ends with a bullet."

"It's my life, I ought to be able to end it any way I see fit."

"And what about mine?"

"Your life is yours, Kate. You do with it what you please."

"And what if I don't want to go with you?"

"If I leave what's left here in the Flat for you, Kate. You going to go back to work?"

Kate Elder stood and glared at Doc Holliday, at a loss for words.

"Let's both think about this, Kate. Nobody's made any decisions yet."

He went out the door and she said, "Yes, they have—yes *you* have, Doc Holliday, even if you don't know it yet."

Wyatt met Holliday at the Griffin Saloon.

"You have any luck finding your man?" Holliday asked.

"No, but I'm still looking."

"What about Adams?"

"He's looking, too. I wish you two would get along better."

"There's something in the air between us. I can feel it whenever we're in the same room together."

"I know. So can I."

Each took a cup of coffee from Mike O'Brien and sat at Holliday's table.

"Clint is also helping Sam Jessup work on the murders of those two girls."

"Uh-huh. Has Adams had experience with that kind of thing?"

"Some. More than Jessup, and I guess more than me. If anybody can find that killer, Clint can."

"You have a lot of respect for him, don't you?"

"More than a lot, Holliday. I think that man is probably the fastest and the smartest man I know."

"He's the fastest you ever saw, then?"

"I think so. I never saw Hickok, so I can't compare them, but I hear they were pretty close."

"That's real interesting."

Wyatt frowned at Holliday and said, "You ain't thinking of changing your mind, are you?"

Holliday shook his head.

"My mind don't work that way, Wyatt. I've got nothing to prove."

"That's good. I'd hate to see two of my friends going up against each other."

"It won't happen."

There was an awkward silence for a few moments, and then Holliday cleared his throat.

"I guess you know there's something I been trying to decide whether or not to tell you."

"I figured."

"Well, I guess I might as well tell you."

"Up to you."

"It might help, and it might be nothing."

Wyatt just waited.

"That man you're looking for, Dave Ruda-baugh."

"Yeah?"

"I've heard O'Brien mention him once or twice in the past."

"Are they friends?"

"I don't think they're friends, exactly, but they know each other."

"And you think O'Brien would know if Ruda-baugh was in town?"

Holliday shrugged and said, "I'm just telling you what I know. For anything else, you'll have to ask Mike."

"He wouldn't be hiding him here in the saloon somewhere, would he?"

"I doubt it. I think I'd know."

"Where, then?"

"Like I said, you'll have to ask him."

Wyatt purposely did not look at O'Brien as he spoke.

"Well, I don't think I'll go right at him about it. I'll have to figure out how to handle it without spooking him."

"Makes sense."

"I appreciate this, Doc," Wyatt said, "no matter how it turns out."

"You find Rudabaugh and you need help taking him, let me know."

"Appreciate that, too."

"Just don't get killed until we settle something."

Wyatt frowned, and then remembered what it was they had to settle. "Don't worry. Before I leave we'll have us a humdinger of a faro game." Holliday nodded and drank his coffee, not looking over at Mike O'Brien.

Now that he had his first real lead to the where-abouts of Dave Rudabaugh, Wyatt Earp didn't want to rush into anything. His respect for Clint Adams was such that he first wanted to discuss the situation with him. He also wanted to see if Clint had anything to add. Between them, and Holliday, he was sure that they'd be able to handle anything that Dave Ruda-baugh threw at them.

Dave Rudabaugh sat inside the steaming hot crib and sweated like a pig. If he had his days figured right, his friend Whit Coughlan ought to arrive in the Flat the next day with a bunch of boys. They were supposed to meet and discuss pulling some jobs in Texas, but Whit and his boys didn't know that Rudabaugh already had a job planned for them, and when it was over they'd be standing while Wyatt Earp, Doc Holliday, that town lawman, and especially Clint Adams, lay face down in the dirt.

And while they were at it, they might as well hit the bank.

Rudabaugh intended to leave the Flat rich and famous, and nobody—not the local law, not the army boys up on the hill, and not Clint Adams, the famous Gunsmith—was going to stop him.

Chapter Twenty-Seven

Somehow Clint and Wyatt managed to miss each other all day. Clint spent quite a bit of time talking to Doctor Gilman—or listening to him—because the man seemed to have a lot of insight into the human mind.

"What else is there to do in a town like this but read?" the man remarked.

As dinner time approached Clint was on his way into his hotel and bumped into Wyatt coming out.

"Where the hell have you been?" Wyatt asked. "I've got some news."

"So have I."

They both started to talk at once, and then both stopped short.

"All right," Clint said, "let's go to that cafe down the street and then you can go first."

They got themselves a table at the cafe, ordered dinner, and then began to talk.

"Doc Holliday finally told me what's been eating at him," Wyatt said.

"Does it help?"

"It might."

Wyatt told Clint what Holliday had said and Clint listened without comment.

"Have you talked to O'Brien yet?" he asked when Wyatt was finished.

"Not yet. I wasn't quite sure how I wanted to handle it and thought we'd talk about it."

"We will," Clint said, "but we'll have to do it later tonight."

"Why not now?"

"Look at this," Clint said, handing Wyatt the telegram from Rick Hartman.

Wyatt read it and passed it back, not looking particularly happy.

"Looks like my man is also Jessup's man."

"Yes, it does."

"What is Jessup planning to do?"

"I've asked him to let you and me work on our ends a little."

"And what's your end?"

Clint told Wyatt how he thought he'd be able to get George Talbot to cooperate with them in a plan to possibly draw Rudabaugh out.

"So Jessup can arrest him?"

"Why don't we get him behind bars, Wyatt, where he can't kill any more girls, and then we can discuss who should get to keep him."

Wyatt stared at Clint a few moments, then said, "You're right, Clint. If he's the killer we have to get him off the streets."

Clint breathed a sigh of relief that his friend had decided to see it his way.

"When are you going to talk to this fella Talbot?" Wyatt asked.

"Tonight."

"His man still on your trail?"

"He's been there all day."

"Want me to get him off?"

"No," Clint said, shaking his head, "I'll just take him along with me."

The waiter brought their food and they ate without tasting. Impatience had robbed them of their appetites.

"It's time to go," Clint said, pushing his seat back to rise.

Wyatt followed his example and asked, "How about I follow the fella who's following you and give you some cover when you go to see Talbot?"

"Good idea. After I've talked to Talbot we'll go back to the hotel and decide on a course of action. I think it's all going to come to a head at the same time, Wyatt."

Clint didn't know at the time how right he was.

They stopped on the boardwalk outside the cafe and, for the bodyguard's benefit, made it look as if they were splitting up. Wyatt walked away and Clint started towards the north end of town. The man across the street stepped out to follow him and did not see Wyatt Earp double back and attach himself to his tail.

Clint Adams felt better knowing that Wyatt Earp was there to watch his back.

Chapter Twenty-Eight

When Clint entered the Red Line Palace it was just as busy as it had been the evening before, even though it was not quite dark yet. Apparently, Talbot had his bodyguards on the lookout because as he started across the floor he walked into one.

"I have an appointment with your boss," Clint said slowly, "remember?"

"You insulted me yesterday," the man said, sullenly.

"Did I?"

"Yeah."

"I don't recall," Clint said. "Which one are you, Deaf, Dumb, Blind, or Just Plain Stupid?"

"I ought to—"

"You ought to take me up to your boss. He won't like being kept waiting, and I'll make sure he knows it was because your feelings were hurt."

The man glared at Clint long enough for the other man, the one who had been following the Gunsmith all day, to enter and move up behind him.

The man in front looked at the man in back and then said to Clint, "Follow me."

"Long as you can find it without getting lost."

161

He saw the man's shoulders tense and followed him to the steps with the other man right behind.

When they reached the second floor they were walking towards Talbot's door when another door opened and Lita Velez appeared. She stopped, surprised to see Clint, who simply smiled at her and winked. She watched the three men as they continued down the hall.

They reached Talbot's door and the bodyguard knocked.

"Come in."

He opened the door and they entered single file, Clint still in the center. Talbot was seated on a divan, smoking a cigar, and the other two bodyguards were present.

"Mr. Adams. Welcome."

"Could you do something about getting this monkey off my back," Clint said. "And maybe you could get him to take a bath. I've been able to smell him all day."

Clint felt the man behind him tense, but Talbot said, "He's right. I can smell you from here. Go and get cleaned up and come right back."

They waited for the man to leave and then the bodyguard who had led Clint up there walked over to one side of the room to join the other two.

"Do you really need those three?"

"Yes."

"Then you've decided not to trust me."

"On the contrary," Talbot said. "I've decided to trust you—but I still need them in the case the killer tries for me before you can get him."

"All right, then we're working together on this."

"Yes."

"Then the first thing I want you to do is get your girls off the street. Don't let them take any customers until this man is caught."

Talbot frowned.

"What will that accomplish, except to cut into my profits?"

"If he can't find a whore he might have to come over the Red Line. If he does, we'll be waiting for him."

"There are other whores out there besides mine."

"Get them off the street, too. Have your girls talk to them."

"They have to make a living—"

"They can't make a living if they're dead. If your girls get off the street they'll be the only ones left. I think they'll understand that."

"All right, we can probably work that out. What comes next?"

"You stay in this room with your bodyguards, just in case the killer is after you, too."

"Makes sense to me."

"I think he'll go looking for a woman, though, before he decides on you. If he does, we'll be able to catch him."

"You're expecting him to come to the decent side of town," Talbot said.

"That's right."

Talbot grinned and said, "How do you think the decent women of this town would react if they knew that you were using them as bait."

"We may not. If it's whores he wants, and not decent women, then he won't come after them."

"And then what do you have?"

"Nothing. We'll have to start all over again."

"Wait a minute," Talbot said, looking as if an idea had occurred to him. "If I get all the whores off the street and he can't find any, maybe he'll just leave town."

"That's not what we want. We want to catch him."

"I want him out of my hair. That's accomplished just as well by his leaving as it would be by your catching him."

"I thought we had a deal, here."

Talbot spread his hands and said, "But I've got a better idea. At least, it suits my purposes better."

"Talbot—"

"All right, all right, I know what you're going to say. A deal is a deal, right? You're right. I'll pull my girls and as many of the other whores off the streets tonight. You are talking about tonight, aren't you?"

"The sooner the better."

"By morning you'll let me know whether or not this worked, right?"

"Or before."

Clint moved to the door but before he reached it it opened and the fourth bodyguard came in. Clint made a show of sniffing the air around him.

"That's a little better. Now instead of smelling like the whole horse, you just smell like the horse's ass."

The bodyguard might have made a move against Clint if it weren't for the look he got from Talbot. After the Gunsmith left all four of the bodyguards started to talk at once, and Talbot cut them all off.

"Relax, all of you," Talbot said after Clint left. "You'll get your shot at the Gunsmith, but we have to take things in order."

"What's first, boss?" one of them asked.

"First is Sheriff Sam Jessup. I want him dead and I want it tonight."

"How do you want it done?"

"I don't care. At this point everyone will just think it's the same killer, anyway. Wait until he's alone, and then do it."

They all started for the door and again Talbot stopped them.

"Not all of you, you idiots. I'll need one of you to stay here with me."

"Which one?" one of them asked.

Talbot examined them all and found little to recommend any of them.

"It really doesn't matter. You decide . . ."

Chapter Twenty-Nine

Dave Rudabaugh was suffering.

At least, part of him was, the part that the real Dave Rudabaugh knew nothing about.

Psychiatrists would have had a field day with Rudabaugh. They would have called him the victim of a mother fixation that had turned to hatred when his mother orphaned him to marry a gambler and go on the road. They would have said that he repressed this hatred for years, and that it had only recently over the past year, begun to surface, resulting in a string of unsolved murders that Dave Rudabaugh knew nothing about.

The other Rudabaugh was the killer, they would have said, which would have mattered little to his victims and his pursuers.

So the other Rudabaugh was suffering because he needed a woman to kill. All Dave Rudabaugh knew was that there was an aching need in his loins for a woman. He also knew that whenever he went out for one he must get so drunk that he never remembered what he did with the woman, or if he even found one. All he knew was that he had skinned knuckles, and the ache in his groin was gone. He translated this into meaning that he had gotten fucked, and then gotten into a fight—if it hadn't happened the other way around.

He wanted to resist tonight, because Whit Coughlan was coming in the next day with his boys, and Rudabaugh didn't want to be hung over.

He laid back on his cot, his arm thrown across his eyes. Maybe if he went to sleep the urge would pass.

The other Rudabaugh smiled, and waited.

Clint met Wyatt outside the Red Line Palace.

"How did it go?"

"Fine. He's going to take all of the whores off the streets."

"How the hell is he going to do that?"

Clint explained his logic and how he felt that Talbot's girls could persuade the others to stay off the streets.

"All right, so what will that accomplish?"

"If this maniac needs a woman bad enough, he's going to have to cross the red line to get one."

"And we'll be waiting for him."

"And if he's Dave Rudabaugh you'll recognize him."

"I've never seen Rudabaugh," Wyatt said, "but yeah, I should be able to recognize him."

"All right, then. Let's go talk to Mike O'Brien, and then to the sheriff."

"If O'Brien up and tells us where Rudabaugh is, we won't have to go through with this plan."

"Let's hope that's the way it happens, Wyatt."

When Clint and Wyatt entered the Griffin Saloon they headed straight for the bar, behind which Mike O'Brien stood. O'Brien, correctly reading their intention, panicked and reached beneath the bar for his shotgun.

"Mike, if you come up with something other than air I'll have to kill you," Wyatt said loudly and firmly.

O'Brien froze, then brought his hand up empty.

"You got somebody who can take over the bar for you?" Wyatt asked.

O'Brien nodded.

"Get 'em."

O'Brien called someone over. Apparently the man was used to spelling him at the bar and asked no questions. O'Brien came out from behind the bar.

"Let's go sit and talk."

They walked him towards the back with Wyatt in front and Clint in the rear. As they passed Doc Holliday's faro table Wyatt said, "You might want to be in on this."

Doc nodded and closed his table in the middle of a game. Nobody complained. From her position at the bar Kate Elder frowned, but stayed put.

Wyatt led O'Brien to Holliday's table and said, "Sit down."

As O'Brien sat Holliday caught up with them and stood by to listen.

"Clint?" Wyatt said, asking Clint Adams if he wanted to handle it.

"Mike, listen carefully. Your friend Dave Rudabaugh has killed two women already and if we don't stop him he's going to kill more."

O'Brien closed his eyes and felt a chill. His fears had been right.

"You knew that, didn't you?"

"I—" O'Brien said, then stopped to moisten his

mouth. "I thought it might be him."

"Why have you been hiding him?"

"I'm afraid of him."

Something occurred to Clint and he asked, "Is that where Belinda was going?"

"Yes."

"You're lucky she didn't get there, Mike. She might be dead now."

"I know."

"Where is he, Mike? Where've you been hiding him?"

Mike O'Brien told them. It was as easy as that.

They collected Sheriff Sam Jessup and the four of them—Clint, Wyatt, Holliday and Jessup—went over the red line to the cribs to find Dave Rudabaugh.

"Which one did he say?" Jessup asked.

It was dark, with only a quarter moon glowing, but Clint thought he'd be able to find the crib from Mike O'Brien's directions.

"Over there," he said. He recognized the area as the one where he'd first seen Belinda Darnell. "That way."

He led them to a small crib made entirely of wood which, in the midst of a bunch of falling down wrecks, seemed sturdy by comparison. It still would have been knocked down by a stiff wind.

Or an impatient man.

"This it?" Jessup asked.

"By my count it is," Clint said. "How do you want to play this?"

"Shit, this madman has been killing people in my town."

Jessup stepped up to a wall of the crib, flexed his heavily muscled arms and pushed. The crib teetered for a moment, then fell over with a crash. The other cribs surrounding them stayed silent and dark.

"Let's see if the bastard's in there!" Jessup said.

The four of them waded in among the fallen timber and began to dig for Dave Rudabaugh.

They came up empty.

"Jesus Christ," Clint said, looking towards the other end of town. "He's out, already."

From behind another crib the three bodyguards—Lou, Curly and Stan—watched.

"There's too many," Lou said.

"We can count, Lou," Curly said.

"What do we do?" Stan watched.

"We wait," Curly said. By default, he had taken on the guise of leader. "We wait for them to split up."

"And if they split into twos?" Stan asked.

"There's three of us," Curly said. "We'll kill them."

"We're going to have to split up," Clint said.

"I'll have to get my deputies," Jessup said. "We've got to cover the town and try to keep the women off the street."

"It's dark," Holliday said, "that shouldn't be hard. Decent women are already off the street."

"Then we'll have to concentrate on the women of the town who aren't decent," Wyatt said.

Clint looked around at the cribs, which normally were lit and noisy, with the whores hawking their wares out front.

"It looks like Talbot's done his part," Clint said. "That means we're left with the saloons in town that are running whores and saloon girls. I'll go with Sam and we'll grab his deputies. We should probably put one or two on the rooftops."

"I've only got two."

"Maybe we can get some of the townsmen to help."

Jessup looked doubtful, but remained silent.

"Doc and I will check out the saloons," Wyatt said.

"We'll meet at the Griffin Saloon. Rudabaugh might try to see O'Brien," Clint said. "Let's move."

They moved away from the fallen cribs, unaware that they were being followed.

"They're splitting into twos, like I said," Stan said, with pride.

"We'll follow the sheriff and Adams. Looks like we're gonna kill two birds with one stone," Curly said.

"Talbot said to make sure Jessup was alone," Lou reminded him.

"Talbot's safe and snug up in his hotel room. Don't worry, when he finds out that they're both dead, he'll pay off. We'll make sure of that."

With their hands on their guns the three bodyguards followed Jessup and Clint as they headed for the jail.

When Dave Rudabaugh entered the crowded Griffin Saloon Mike O'Brien saw him immediately and his blood froze. He reached underneath the bar for the shotgun, but his hand wouldn't close over it.

Rudabaugh approached the bar and looked at O'Brien as if he didn't know him.

"Where's the whore?" Rudabaugh asked the bartender. These places always had whores. It was odd, though, how he hadn't been able to find one by the cribs.

The bartender's eyes widened and he said, "Up-upstairs. First door on the right."

Rudabaugh moved through the crowd, not hearing them, only thinking about the whore upstairs.

Chapter Thirty

The first shot struck Jessup high on the left shoulder as they were approaching the jail.

"Shit!" he yelled out.

"Down!" Clint shouted, grabbing Jessup's good shoulder and pulling him down. There were some more shots, all of which went over their heads, but enough to tell them that there was more than one person shooting at them.

"How bad?" Clint asked.

"Not bad enough," Jessup said. "Do you think it's him?"

"Only if he's got friends in town crazy enough to kill a lawman."

"Who, then?" Jessup asked.

"I might take a guess."

Jessup looked at him in the darkness and said, "George Talbot?"

"His so-called bodyguards. Why not? If you get killed won't the townspeople be quick to blame it on the same crazy killer? What's Talbot got to lose? He's taking his best shot to get rid of you."

"Well, it's not going to be good enough. When I get through here I'm going after that weasel."

"Let's just get through here, first," Clint reminded him.

He stuck his head up to draw some fire and then ducked down as a hail of bullets came.

"How many you figure?" Jessup asked.

"Two, maybe three. I'll say three and Talbot kept one in the room with him."

"Where are they?"

"Across the street."

"We're pinned down."

"So what? If they move we'll see them. They're just as pinned down as we are. Now let's see who's got the most patience."

After they split from Clint and Jessup, Holliday put his hand on Wyatt's shoulder.

"I want to go to O'Brien's now."

Wyatt frowned, then said, "Kate?"

"I want to make sure she's okay."

"All right, let's go."

When they reached the Griffin Saloon the music and noise inside was loud enough so that they didn't hear the shots coming from near the sheriff's office.

Kate Elder was standing at the bar and they pushed through the crowd to get to her.

"I'm taking you home," Holliday said.

"Why?"

"To keep you safe."

"From what?"

"Come on, Kate," Wyatt said. "We'll explain on the way."

As Wyatt took her arm his eyes fell on Mike O'Brien, who was slumped against the bar, sweating profusely and looking like a man in shock. Quickly, feeling something was wrong, Wyatt looked around.

"What's wrong, Wyatt?" Holliday asked.

"Something's wrong. Look at O'Brien."

Holliday did and said, "He looks like he's seen a ghost."

Wyatt turned to Kate and said, "What happened here?"

"Nothing. I saw a man go over to him and Mike did look kind of scared."

"Where'd the man go?"

"He headed upstairs. I guess Mike told him where Belinda's room—"

"He's given him the girl, Doc!" Holliday shouted, and both men ran towards the stairs.

Rudabaugh turned the doorknob and walked in. The whore was sitting in front of a mirror, admiring herself as all whores did. They all thought they were perfect, that because they had a beautiful body and face they could do anything and get away with it.

Well, he was the instrument that proved them wrong.

She saw his reflection in the mirror as he closed the door behind him and locked it, and she turned in surprise.

"Who the hell—"

He smiled and said, "Hello, Mother."

Chapter Thirty-One

"We can't just sit here all night," Sam Jessup said. "For one thing I might bleed to death."

"I thought you said it wasn't bad?"

"It's not *bad*. It hurts like hell and it's bleeding, but it's not *bad*."

In the darkness Clint couldn't see Jessup's face well enough to judge whether the man was lying or not. His tone was steady, but if his face had been waxy and sweating, the wound would have been a bad one. Clint decided to take the man at his word.

"All right, then. You don't want to outwait them?"

"No. I want to know what's happening in other parts of town."

"Have it your way, then. You go right and I'll go left. I'd say they were fanned out across the street near the General Store and the Cafe."

"I'd say you were right."

"On three."

"Right."

"Ready? One . . . two . . . three!"

They both sprang into action and by the pause that came just before the shots they knew they'd caught

179

their opposition by surprise. Also, the shots were hurried and way off the mark. Maybe this wouldn't be too hard, after all.

Clint was on his own, now. He couldn't see Jessup and he could play off him. He assumed the same held true for the sheriff.

He kept moving, figuring they'd split up to go after him and the sheriff.

He was wrong and it took him only a moment to figure it out.

They were all firing at Jessup.

He reversed his direction and ran across the street to get behind them. If they were indeed Talbot's bodyguards, then his original estimate of their brain power was intact. They were acting as if he were still running for his life and were concentrating on Jessup alone, who must have been pinned down again.

He could see their dark shapes and the flashes of their guns. To call out to them would be foolish, giving them a chance to shoot at him. He disliked shooting men from behind, but bushwackers did not deserve much better.

He fired once and heard someone howl in pain. The others turned to face him and fired. He ducked into a doorway and saw the flash of Jessup's gun. Another man went down, leaving only one left.

And he wasn't having anymore.

He ran out into the street in plain sight where either Clint or Jessup could have killed him, and then started running. From his direction they guessed he was heading for the livery stable, and away from them and from George Talbot.

Neither of them fired.

They met over the bodies of the other two and

Clint bent over to examine them.

"They're Talbot's men, all right."

"That bastard's finally made a mistake."

"How's your shoulder?"

"Not bad," Jessup said, moving it experimentally. "I think the bullet gouged a piece out and kept going."

Clint could see Jessup's face now and his eyes looked clear. He didn't look like a man in shock from a serious wound.

"Where were your deputies when we needed them?"

"Probably making their rounds. We can find them—"

"Forget it. Let's get over to O'Brien's and meet the others."

"After that," Jessup said with some satisfaction, "Talbot . . ."

"What room is hers?" Wyatt asked Holliday.

"First on the right."

Wyatt, in the lead, turned right and tried the doorknob. It was locked.

"Belinda!" Holliday shouted, joining her.

"Let's break it down."

They both put their shoulders to the door and it sprang open. On the floor lay Belinda Darnell, half naked, some blood on her lower lip and chin—but she was alive. Her breasts were naked and heaving as she fought for breath. Her window was open and while Holliday bent over her Wyatt looked out over the main street.

He saw a shadowy figure jump to the ground, and then saw Clint and Jessup coming from the other direction. For a moment he thought about not yelling, for that would give Jessup the edge on catching him, but then he thought about the dead women.

"There he goes, north on the main street!"

Holliday was behind him then saying, "The girl's fine. Let's go."

Kate Elder had entered the room and taken the girl from Holliday, and now she watched both men climb out the window.

"Be careful, Doc!" she shouted.

Clint and Jessup heard Wyatt's yell and saw the figure running away from them.

"There he goes," Clint said. "Come on let's not lose him."

They started running after him and it soon became apparent where he was heading.

"He doesn't know we found his crib," Clint said. "He's heading for his hiding place."

"If we lose him among the cribs . . ." Jessup said, and then both men shut up and preserved their energy for running.

Dave Rudabaugh was confused.

The last he remembered he was lying on the cot in his crib, and then suddenly he was in that woman's room, pawing her breasts. Someone had banged on the door then and he gave in to instinct and ran.

He was confused, though. How had he gotten there? Had he gotten drunk and gone to the woman's room with her? But he didn't feel drunk, not at all.

And who was chasing him?

He ran back across the red line to the cribs and stopped short when he saw that his had been destroyed somehow. Had he done that, too?

He looked around frantically for a place to hide but all the cribs were shut tight. That didn't make sense. This had been the perfect place to hide because men were always coming and going to make use of the women in the cribs.

He heard footsteps behind him and ran among the cribs, trying doors in a blind panic, looking for one he could force.

Clint and Jessup stopped running when they reached the cribs and looked around.

"By now he knows his is gone," Clint said.

"Where is he? In one of these?"

"We can't knock them all down."

Wyatt Earp and Doc Holliday caught up to them.

"Where is he?" Wyatt asked.

"In there, somewhere," Clint said. "What happened back there?"

"He got to the woman, Belinda."

"Is she all right?"

"He beat her up some, but she's all right," Holliday said. "We're going to have to fan out if we're going to find him."

"We'll find him, all right," Wyatt said.

"I want him, Earp," Jessup said. "He's killed two women—"

"We can talk about that later," Clint said, interrupting. "Let's find him first, before we fight over who gets him."

The others agreed and they spread out and went their separate ways, looking for him.

Dave Rudabaugh knew he'd done some bad things in his life, but he didn't know what he'd done that these men were after him. Could it be for beating up a whore? Why would they want him so badly for that?

From his hiding place behind a crib he saw four men split up and he knew he could hide from them, and he couldn't take them all.

Backing up he banged into a crib door that gave slightly. He turned, kicked out and the door splintered. Inside, a lamp came on and he went in.

The woman on the cot was past her prime, a blowsy, fortyish blonde with plump breasts and a fleshy face.

"You want it that bad, Johnny?" she asked.

This one, he thought suddenly, this one *looks* like his mother.

"Bitch!" the other Rudabaugh said, and drew his gun.

The woman screamed and covered her face.

Clint was nearest when they all heard the splintering wood of the kicked-in door. The light acted like a beacon and he turned in that direction. He saw Rudabaugh framed in the doorway, heard him shout "Bitch!" and draw his gun. The Gunsmith drew, and as the woman screamed, he fired.

Dave Rudabaugh felt something punch him in the small of his back and all the air went out of his lungs.

He died, wondering what he was dying for.

A man has a right to know that, doesn't he?

Chapter Thirty-Two

While Clint and Jessup went up to see George Talbot, Wyatt and Holliday stayed on the steps, in case anyone from downstairs wanted to deal themselves in.

"This time he's gone too far," Jessup said in the hall, "and I've got him."

They stopped in front of Talbot's door and were about to knock when there was a shot from inside.

"Damn!" Jessup said. They hit the door together and it sprang open.

Estralita Velez was standing in the center of the room holding a small gun on a cowering George Talbot. From Clint's vantage point the gun looked like a .32. In the corner the fourth bodyguard was lying on the floor with a hole in his chest, very dead.

"No more," Lita was saying, "you will hit me and control my life no more."

Talbot saw Clint and Jessup and said, "Sheriff, thank God you're here. This woman's gone crazy."

"Lita—" Clint said.

She recognized his voice without turning her head.

"I thought about what you said, Clint," she said,

"about doing something for myself. This is the thing I must do to be free."

"Sheriff, do your duty," Talbot shouted. He was sitting on his divan, shaking and sweating and staring at the barrel of Lita's gun. "Shoot her!"

"Hijo de un cabrone!" Lita spat at him.

"Lita—" Clint said, starting forward, but Jessup grabbed his arm and held him. Lita's gun went off twice and her aim was true. She shot him first in the crotch, and then in the head. In death, Talbot's eyes refused to close, staring ahead in disbelief.

Clint looked at Jessup and shook off the man's strong hold.

"Cleaner this way, Clint," Jessup said. "Neater for everyone concerned." He walked to Lita and took the gun away from her. "A clear case of self defense."

He took Lita gently by the arm, turned her and walked her to Clint.

"Did you really tell her that?" Jessup asked.

"Yes."

The sheriff turned to look at Talbot's body, then looked back at the Gunsmith and said, "Damn good advice."

Wyatt Earp left the Flat the following morning secure in the knowledge that he would get paid the full amount he was entitled to. Sam Jessup was wiring the railroad that Rudabaugh had been killed by Earp. Clint Adams had agreed to that.

Doc Holliday and Kate Elder left the Flat some days later, heading for Dodge City, where Wyatt Earp had said he'd probably end up after reporting back to the railroad.

Sam Jessup didn't know it, but a group of men led by Whit Coughlan arrived in the Flat that day, stayed for two days waiting for Dave Rudabaugh and, when he didn't put in an appearance, left to look for other banks to rob.

Clint Adams said goodbye to Lita and Belinda the next morning and left the Flat, heading for Labyrinth, Texas. Belinda had agreed to take Lita under her wing. Though not fully in control of her own life, she felt that together they might be able to break away from the Flat and start fresh somewhere.

The Gunsmith wished them luck—and envied them the second chance.

GREAT BOOKS

E-BOOKS

AUDIOBOOKS

& MORE

Visit us today

www.speakingvolumes.us

Made in the USA
Las Vegas, NV
14 July 2021

26454916R00114